Crossing
the Mangrove

Also by Maryse Condé

Heremakhonon
A Season in Rihata
Segu
Children of Segu
I, Tituba, Black Witch of Salem
Tree of Life

Translated by
Richard Philcox

Anchor Books
A Division of
Random House, Inc.
New York

*Crossing
the Mangrove*

Maryse Condé

First Anchor Books Edition, March 1995

Originally published as Traversée de la mangrove *by Mercure de France,*
copyright © 1989 by Mercure de France
Translation copyright © 1995 by Doubleday, a division of Random House, Inc.

Library of Congress Cataloging-in-Publication Data

Condé, Maryse.
    [Traversée de la mangrove.   English]
    Crossing the Mangrove / Maryse Condé ; translated by Richard Philcox.
        p.   cm.
    1. Guadeloupe—Social life and customs—Fiction.   I. Philcox, Richard.
II. Title.
PQ3949.2.C65T7313   1995
843—dc20   *94-35504*
                                                              CIP

ISBN 0-385-47633-7

Book design by Terry Karydes

www.anchorbooks.com

Printed in the United States of America
20 19 18 17 16 15 14

Translator's Preface

As Tituba says in Maryse Condé's *I, Tituba, Black Witch of Salem*, "I took a long time making up my mind . . . I made comparisons, I fingered and prodded and finally I found her . . ."

Just like Tituba, I the translator of *Crossing the Mangrove* took a long time making up my mind how to go about translating this novel. What was I going to do with all those Creole expressions? How was I going to render this most Guadeloupean of Maryse Condé's novels into English? How was I going to translate those distortions of the French language that Creole is so fond of making and at the same time poke fun at standard, academic French? I could have researched the English-speaking West Indian equivalents of many Creole expressions, but this would have distanced the reader from the French and Creole-speaking environment of Guadeloupe and transported him or her to Barbados or Jamaica. I could have invented words in English (I did in one or two cases) but I (and even less the author) have no quarrel with the English language on the same level as Creole quibbles with French.

No, I decided to concentrate on the tone and register of these voices speaking from this wake ceremony and talking to us, even chatting to us, as we turn the pages. I looked everywhere for that right tone, trying to get a voice or voices that spoke to me of the inner, psychological drama being enacted in each and every one of these characters.

I opened James Joyce's *Ulysses* and the Irishness of his voice cried out from between the pages. I leafed through Faulkner's *As I Lay Dying* and the accent of the American South lilted out. I delved into V. S. Naipaul and found I was on the wrong island. I even looked at Gabriel García Márquez's short story "Leaf Storm" about a wake ceremony, but nothing seemed appropriate. And then I found it. In a most unlikely place. And yet not so unlikely, because I had already sensed it in Maryse Condé's second novel, *A Season in Rihata*. I found that tone and register of voice, those trifling details with universal significance, the way the colors of Nature interweave in personal lives and the way the reader is made to look at the horizon and then back again to him or herself. I found all this in Virginia Woolf, and in particular in her novel *To the Lighthouse*. Her stream of consciousness technique spoke to me as a translator. I like the way the narrator slips in and out of the characters' lives and talks to us in a voice that touches the right chord. You might be wondering how the register for an English middle-class family could be appropriate for the inhabitants of a small village in Guadeloupe. It is because I sense a similarity of purpose and a mastery of style in both authors that transcends the two very different contexts of a holiday home on the English coast and a tropical village.

So it was with Virginia Woolf's voice in the back of my head that I set about translating *Crossing the Mangrove* and rendering that *sound* and *conviction* of both writers. Both discourses are very close to each other and both texts fill the characters and the reader with renewed energy and hope.

The translator would like to express warmest thanks to Sue Lanser from the University of Maryland for her comments, suggestions and encouragement.

This translation has been supported by a grant from the National Endowment for the Humanities, an independent federal agency.

Contents

For Richard

Dusk

"My heart did not tell me! My heart did not tell me!"

Mademoiselle Léocadie Timothée, a retired elementary school teacher for over twenty years, stood with one hand on her breast, the other rolled into a cone level with her mouth, and went over her dreams in slow motion, taking herself back to that night the previous week when the pain of her worn-out body, together with the barking of Leo's dogs next door and the lowing of his cows tied up in the savanna next to her house, had kept her awake until four in the morning, the hour when the pale and timid light of dawn had already stolen noiselessly between her louvered windows. No. Nothing had emerged from the opaque waters of sleep. As usual, ever since she had moved deeper into the depths of old age, she had dreamt of her sister who had died without experiencing the vicissitudes of marriage and the joys of motherhood like herself; she had dreamt of her mother who had experienced both, and there the two of them were, back in good health before their sickness and suffering, looking as young as ever, waiting for her at the open gates to Eternal Life.

No doubt about it: it was him.

Face down in the sticky mud with his clothes soiled, his heavy-built frame and curly mop of salt and pepper hair were easily recognizable.

The smell was appalling and Mademoiselle Léocadie Timothée, who had a sensitive heart and stomach, was disgusted at herself for feeling sick. She retched and then knelt down on both knees in the tall Guinea grass on the bank and vomited. Like all the villagers of Rivière au Sel she had hated the man who now lay at her feet. But death being what it is, when it passes by, respect it.

She crossed herself three times, lowered her head and recited the prayer for the dead. Then she looked around her, frightened out of her wits. What had gotten into her to cut off along this forest path she had never taken before? What had pushed her to stumble with both feet on this corpse? Every day, once dusk fell, she turned the key to the house where she lived alone, surrounded by memories, photographs, dozing cats, and birds who built their nests in the hollows of her lampshades, and went out to take the air, walking along a straight unswerving line from the Villa Perety, thirty years earlier as lovely as a picture, today dilapidated under trees eaten by creepers, abandoned by its owners who preferred to live in French France, to the Lameaulnes Nurseries whose entrance was barred by an iron gate and a sign saying "Private Property." Today she had taken a different path. What had been more powerful than years and years of habit?

Forcing her old body, spurring it with the terror that was now boiling inside her, she made her way back to the village. With her heart racing, thumping in her ears, she climbed back up the forest track and found the footpath between the ferns, now dark owing to the late hour, that came out on the road at the chapel to the Virgin Mary, Mother of All Sorrows.

The dead man's house stood just outside the village, hemmed in by the forest that had begrudgingly left an opening of several miles and was anxious in its greed to win back the lost ground. The house was made of corrugated iron and wooden planks, even though throughout the island even the poorest were striving to build with concrete under the new tax incentive laws. It was obvious that the man had not cared what other people might think. In his eyes a house was a place where you ate, where you sheltered from the rain and where you lay down to sleep. Two dogs, two Dobermans, their coats the color of Satan, who had been seen feasting on innocent chickens, rushed out, barking and baring their cruel ivory-colored fangs. Mademoiselle Léocadie stopped therefore at the gate, raising her broken voice with a cautious "Anyone at home?"

A teenager emerged, his face drawn tight as a prison door. "Down! Down!" he shouted at the animals. And the monsters withdrew, sensing a more violent presence than themselves.

"Is she there, Alix?" Mademoiselle Léocadie asked, still not moving.

The teenager nodded. Aroused by all this ruckus, Vilma herself came out onto the veranda. Mademoiselle Léocadie decided to go in. How was she to announce to this young thing, this child she had seen christened one fine Sunday in August—oh how she could remember it—that her man was lying in the mud, as dead as a doornail! Mademoiselle Léocadie had never imagined that one day the Good Lord to whom she prayed so devoutly, missing neither Vespers nor Rosary nor the month of May, would send her such a cross to bear, such a tribulation at the end of her old age.

"He didn't come home to sleep, did he?" she stammered.

Vilma did not even think of lying, and with her eyes damp from the warm salty tears of sorrow she uttered an explanation: "Nor the night before, nor the night before that. It's been three nights. I'm scared. Maman has sent Alix to sleep with me in case my pains come."

Mademoiselle Léocadie plucked up her courage. "Let me come in, I have something to tell you."

Inside they sat down on either side of the whitewood table and Mademoiselle Léocadie began to talk. So it was that the warm salty tears overflowed from Vilma's eyes and streamed down her cheeks, still chubby from childhood. Tears of pain, tears of mourning, but not of surprise. For she had known from the very start that this man would break into and out of her life in a brutal fashion.

When Mademoiselle Léocadie had finished speaking, Vilma did not move, slumped in her chair as if the grief was too much for her eighteen-year-old shoulders. Then she turned to Alix, who had come in during the conversation, no doubt attracted by that special smell of calamity.

"Did you hear?" she asked.

He again nodded. It was clear that the only pain he felt was the one hurting his sister.

"Go and tell Father!" Vilma ordered.

Alix obeyed.

Outside, the night had crept in on tiptoe. The mountain ridge could no longer be seen silhouetted against the sky beyond the black foliage of the mahogany trees. Electric light shone from every cabin and radios bawled the news without managing to drown the cries of children. Amid a jabber of words and gibberish, the men were drinking their white rum at Chez Christian while the players slammed down their dice on the wooden tables. All this noise and commotion shocked Alix; after all, a man was lying dead on a muddy path, even if it was a man for whom not an eye, except perhaps Vilma's and Mira's, would shed a tear. He entered the noise and cigarette smoke and with authority clapped his hands. Usually nobody would have paid any attention to this young pup. But such was his expression as he stood at the corner of the counter that they guessed the nature of the words soon to be uttered before he had even opened his mouth. Black and oppressive like mourning. So it was amid complete silence that he announced:

"Francis Sancher is dead!"

"Dead?" the men repeated.

Those who were sitting got up in disorder, the others stood transfixed.

Without another word, Alix turned his back. He knew the question that was about to follow and for which he did not yet have an answer.

"Who killed him?"

While he strode in haste towards his parents' house, the men, forgetting their rum and dice, hurried off to spread the news to the four corners of the village, and soon people were crowding on their doorsteps to comment on the matter, not in the least surprised, however, for everybody knew full well that one day Francis Sancher would come to a bad end!

Alix's announcement staggered its way through the mind of Moïse the postman, nicknamed Mosquito, not because he was drunk, as was common one evening out of three, but because he had been the first in Rivière au Sel to make Francis Sancher's acquaintance at the very moment he had stepped off the bus and asked the way to the Alexis property, even though now every time Francis's name was mentioned it made him spit and side with Sancher's worst enemies. Once its meaning had become clear and reached the farthest corner of his brain he started to shake like a leaf on a branch on days when the wind gets up. So Francis had been right to be frightened! His implacable enemy had smelled him out, tracked him down and struck in the very oasis of greenery where he had come to bury himself! It was not therefore the deep-rooted, crazy, superstitious terror that had seemed so surprising in a man of his stature. He stood up heavily, his heartbeats shaking his puny frame. Then he ran out after Alix.

The moon closed its two golden eyes when they rolled over the massive body of Francis Sancher, his swollen face turned upwards. The stars did likewise. No light filtered down from the silent sky.

Lowering their lighted torches Alix and Alain shed light over their older brothers, Carmélien and Jacques, kneeling in the awful smell. Their father, Sylvestre Ramsaran, was standing a little way back, Moïse blending in with his shadow. Carmélien looked up and whispered:

"There's no blood on him!"

"No blood?"

The six men looked at each other in astonishment. Then without further ado Jacques slid the corpse onto the bamboo stretcher and motioned to his brothers to help him. The procession set off. The timid moon then opened its eyes again and lit up every corner of the landscape.

When the procession reached Vilma's house a crowd had gathered in the lane, in the garden and on the veranda, half in mourning, half curious for news. There were those who were directly involved—Rosa, Vilma's mother; Loulou Lameaulnes, the owner of the nurseries; Dinah, his second wife from Saint-Martin; Aristide, Loulou's only son who had stayed behind to work in Rivière au Sel; and Joby, the first child from his second marriage, a pale little boy who had been confirmed the year before. Mira, of course, was not there, and it would have surprised, even shocked people if she had been. Yet, except for Emmanuel Pélagie, who as soon as he got back from Dillon would lock his Peugeot in his garage and not even come out on his veranda to take the air, the whole of Rivière au Sel was there. Even Sonny, the unfortunate Sonny, even Désinor the Haitian . . .

Seeing such a crowd you might have concluded they were being hypocritical. For all of them, at one time or another, had called Francis a vagabond and a cur, and isn't the fate of a cur to die amid general indifference?

Actually, people had come mainly out of respect for Vilma's parents, the Ramsarans, one of the most esteemed families in Rivière au Sel. After having laid up his father with a vicious kick for three long months in a hospital bed in La Pointe for refusing to give him sugarcane cuttings, Ti-Tor Ramsaran, Vilma's great-grandfather, had put as much distance as he could between himself and his bad deed and had settled in this region of the island— an unusual spot for an East Indian—the same year as Gabriel, the first of the Lameaulnes, a white Creole from Martinique, who had been hounded out by his family because he married a Negress. This must have been in 1904 or 1905. In any case before the 1914–1918 war and well before the hurricane of 1928.

When Ti-Tor turned up, quite a few people took offense and chanted spitefully: "Kouli malaba isi dan pa peyiw!" (Coolie malabar, this country's not yours!) But Ti-Tor ignored them and kept his eyes glued on the four acres of land he had purchased. These four acres had led to more land for the next generation when the Farjol factory had closed down and the land had been sold off in parcels. Rodrigue, Ti-Tor's son, had bought forty acres and planted them with bananas, since the island no longer had any use for sugarcane. The old people, who had been through the First World War, shook their heads.

"What's got into the place? If cane goes, Guadeloupe goes!"

Many were angry with Rodrigue's purchase and complained:

"Since when do the Indians lay down the law around here?"

For the Ramsarans were getting richer and Rodrigue had replaced the wooden cabin where he had come into this world with a one-story, reinforced concrete villa girded by a balustraded balcony in wrought iron that he called L'Aurélie.[1]

L'Aurélie? Where did that name come from?

Nevertheless, the envious and the discontented soon went into real fits of rage when Carmélien, Rodrigue's grandson and the son of Sylvestre, went to study medicine in France. What! A Ramsaran, a doctor! People don't know their place! The Ramsarans' place was on the land, cane or no cane! Fortunately, God works in mysterious ways! Carmélien quickly returned home from Bordeaux when he came down with an illness. There is justice in this world. You shouldn't get too big for your breeches. In such cases life does its duty and brings the overly ambitious back to earth.

People hadn't finished deriding Carmélien, nicknaming him "Doktè," before he had two ponds dug on his father's land and had started breeding crayfish. People who as children had fished them by hand from the rivers' icy pools, began by asserting that these artificial crayfish were not worth the peppers and chives they

---

[1] *The name of the first ship to bring indentured East Indians to Guadeloupe.*

were seasoned with, but they were silenced when all the hotels for tourists from as far away as Le Gosier and Saint-François put in their orders, which Carmélien delivered in a Toyota pickup, and one evening right on Télé-Guadeloupe itself, between the habitual epithets for products made in France, appeared a commercial that bellowed out: "Dinners for special occasions. Business lunches. Weddings. Banquets. Buy local. Buy Ramsaran crayfish."

The person this sickened and irritated the most in Rivière au Sel was Loulou Lemeaulnes who, like his parents and grandparents before him, played the aristocrat behind the nurseries' iron gate, which in season was covered with mauve and orange flowers from the Julie creeper and trumpet hibiscus. He too had thought of a TV commercial for his flowers and plants. Then he had told himself that was white folks' ways and better left to them. And now along comes this upstart Carmélien who had been born the same year as Kléber, his second boy, and goes one better than him.

Despite these petty tensions, bitterness and jealousies, the Ramsarans were a respected family, always attending ceremonies, never begrudging a sizable contribution for the annual feast day or the carnival procession. Although some of them had never intermarried and gone off to the Grands Fonds from where they originated to find a partner, many of them had married into black or mulatto families in the region. And so were related by blood to much of Rivière au Sel.

It was around nine and the moon was resting behind an ink-colored cloud which was getting ready, so it seemed, to burst, and Monsieur Démocrite, the school's principal, had sent for the tarpaulin that was used to cover the football field, when Dr. Martin arrived from Petit-Bourg at the wheel of his luxurious BMW and locked himself up for a long tête-à-tête with the corpse. When he emerged nothing was written on his face. He went and telephoned from Dodose Pélagie's, who stood in vain behind the door to catch the conversation. Despite appearances, even if there were no blood or wounds on the corpse, this apparently was no natural death. Around 10 p.m. therefore an ambulance rolled up scattering the idlers with its siren, and for three days and three nights the body of Francis Sancher hung around on the cold marble tops of autopsy tables until a doctor was called from La Pointe as a last resort and was categorical: We should not let the talk of rum-besotted villagers go to our heads. We should not look for difficulties where there are none. Aneurysmal rupture. This sort of accident is common with hot-blooded individuals who overstep their quota of alcohol.

So on the afternoon of the fourth day Francis Sancher came back home, no longer on his solid two feet and a head above the rest, even the tallest, but laid out in the light-varnished wooden prison of a coffin with a glass plate on top so you could see his square, handsome face for a few hours longer. The coffin was placed on the bed, covered with a profusion of fresh flowers from the nurseries, in the larger of the two bedrooms under the three beams symbolizing Bread, Wine and Poverty,[2] which during his lifetime had witnessed Francis Sancher's prolific lovemaking with his succession of women, and which had never been touched by a broom. While the men remained seated on benches, laughing and joking under Monsieur Démocrite's tarpaulin, sheltering from the rain that poured through the sky's leaky roof, the women busied themselves cooking thick soup with the beef that the Ramsarans, wealthy cattle breeders from the Grands Fonds, had brought for their relatives in mourning, serving rounds of white rum and

---

[2] *A way of predicting the fate of a home by counting the beams that represent Bread = strict minimum, Wine = abundance, and Poverty = misfortune.*

arranging themselves in a pious circle around the death bed to recite prayers.

About four, Mira turned up; she had not been seen since giving birth and was back to being the dazzling beauty she had been before she was shamed, thinner nevertheless, walking studiedly as if she were fighting with her heart and having great difficulty controlling its leaps and bounds. When she entered, every head looked up, every eye stared, every finger forgot to roll its rosary beads. How was she going to react in front of the girl who had slipped into the same bed? However, anybody who was hoping for a sacrilegious scandal at such a moment, who was already imagining a shocking scene to recount during the evenings to come, was in for a disappointment. Mira looked neither left nor right, but merely stared with an infinite compassion devoid of anger at the face that had rejected her, then took her place among the pious circle of worshipers who intoned:

"For everything its season, and for every activity under heaven its time: a time to be born and a time to die; a time to plant and a time to uproot; a time to kill and a time to heal; a time for mourning and a time for dancing; a time to scatter stones and a time to gather them."

The sky started to darken.

Shortly after Mira came Lucien Evariste, commonly known as the Writer, although he had never written a word, and Emile Etienne, commonly known as the Historian, although he had only published one pamphlet that nobody ever read entitled "Let's Talk About Petit-Bourg"; the first arrived from Petit-Bourg by the bus "Christ the King," whose driver made a detour and shut off the engine to come to a silent halt under the roof of trees while he hurriedly crossed himself; the second drove up in his familiar Peugeot. They had both been great friends of Francis Sancher's, which was of no surprise in the case of Lucien, a hothead who had broken his mother's heart, but certainly was in the case of Emile whose profession should have prompted him to be more responsible.

When did they notice the presence of Xantippe, huddled up in the corner of the veranda, motionless, silent, eyes glowing like cinders under a cooking pot? How long had he been there? When had he arrived? No one could say. It was just like him to slip in unnoticed. Like when he settled in on the edge of Rivière au Sel. Shortly after Francis Sancher's arrival, one October when the rains never let up. Then one day he had been seen quietly fixing poles in his yam patch and people knew he was living at the crossroads in Bois Sec in a hovel where two charcoal burners, Justinien and Josyna, used to take shelter once a month to burn logwood, before the Butagaz company killed their business.

The hovel was pieced together with sheets of corrugated iron and had a low ceiling, the only light coming in through a single opening. How could a human being take refuge there? Xantippe's presence always created a real malaise. Immediately, the noise stopped in an icy sea of silence and some thought of shouldering him out. But you don't lock the door to a wake. It remains wide open for all and sundry to surge in. Soon, therefore, some of the men resumed their joking and laughter. Others in silence started to think of Francis Sancher, sucking on their memories like a hollow tooth.

Outside, tied to the mahogany trees, the two Dobermans, who had been devoted to their master and whom nobody had thought to feed, howled continuously from hunger and despair.

And the moon shone grandly from behind the damp curtain of rain.

The Night

Moïse the Postman, Known as Mosquito

"I was the first to know his real name."

Moïse repeated the words to himself as if they gave him a right to the deceased, a right he was unwilling to share with either of the two women who had loved Francis or with the two children he had planted in their wombs, one who was already shooting up fatherless under the sun, the other who was getting ready to enter this world as an orphan with nothing but two eyes to cry with.

He also believed he was one of the few people to know

why Francis had chosen to shut himself up in this little island calabash tossed by the ocean's bad temper. Not that Francis had let him into the slightest secret. Oh no! He thought he had caught a glimpse of the truth through the flow of virtually incomprehensible words Francis would let loose every evening when, once they had drunk to saturation point at Chez Christian, they would return home and drink the remainder of the night away until the sun loomed up between the mountains signaling the approach of first light. When he was with Francis, Moïse kept his mouth shut. First of all, because Francis did not listen to him. Secondly, because anything he would have said, or even invented, would have seemed pale and insipid compared to the spicy plates of fantasies that Francis, always brimming over with words, dished up day after day.

Before he met Francis, Moïse was always chattering on about how the women were barring him from their hearts and beds, how the men were ridiculing him and how, as time went by, his dreams had withered like a tree during the dry season.

After meeting him, he began to think that life would take on a new meaning and that leaves would bud on the tree of tomorrow.

Until the day when he had to come to terms with the fact that he had worked himself up for no reason, that Francis was nothing but a creature with nowhere to turn burrowing himself in at the bottom of a hole to die! He recalled that noon, splashed with light, when he had seen him for the first time. He was finishing his daily morning round from the post office at Petit-Bourg to the Trou au Chien, then to Mombin, Dillon, Petite-Savane, Rousses, and Bois l'Etang, ending at Rivière au Sel where he had his own place and even a garage built of planks to house the yellow postal van. A postman, he's everybody's man.

After drinking shots of straight rum at every house he stopped at, either to pay out the money orders mailed by the children in French France or to hand over the mail order catalogs from Les Trois Suisses or La Redoute in Roubaix, he was a bit tipsy, not really drunk, just enough to forget the old wounds and race along the roads singing and honking his horn.

It was then he saw this burly, heavy-built man as tall as a mahogany tree crowned with a mass of curly, graying hair talking to Madame Mondésir, who was standing on her veranda. By Madame Mondésir's face you could guess what she was thinking. Where did this man spring from? Do you answer questions from somebody whom you've never set eyes on before? Finally, the mahogany tree started to move off, bumping along the tarmac a green metal trunk on wheels. Moïse stepped on the accelerator and, when he caught up with him, shouted:

"Sa ou fè? Ola ou kaye kon sa?" (Hi! Where are you off to?)

The stranger gave him a look of incomprehension, which settled for Moïse at least one point: This was not a Guadeloupean, for even the Negropolitans[3] who have been yellowing their hides for years from the sunless winters of the Paris suburbs know what these words mean. Moïse continued:

"Climb aboard! The sun's hot! Where are you heading for?"

"Do you know the Alexis house?"

The Alexis house? Moïse thought he had misheard. Then it seemed to him an excellent augur that this man's first words formed a bold, unusual question as well as a challenge. He opened the van door.

"Climb aboard!" he repeated.

It was in the 1950s, perhaps a bit before, just after the end of the war, once the Alexis boy had laid his parents to rest, that he sold off their entire assets bought with the fine salaries of two top-

---

[3] *French West Indians who have lived most of their lives in metropolitan France.*

grade elementary school teachers. He didn't have problems finding a buyer for their upstairs-downstairs house in Petit-Bourg, situated just opposite the fire station, into which moved the young doctor Tiburce, straight from the hospital in Toulouse. But as for the "change of air" house in Rivière au Sel set amid a 30,000 square foot orchard the deceased had planted with orange and grapefruit trees and which gave the sweetest, sugary litchis—no such luck. The "House for Sale" sign remained for years on end soaking up sun and rain, until one day it fell to the ground in pieces and was forgotten.

To begin with, the Alexis estate seemed a godsend. In the mango season, the children on their way home from school would make a detour to take aim with their stones at the Julie and Amélie mangoes. The poor would pole down the breadfruit for their migan[4] or pick the green bananas for their pot of tripe. At Christmas, pigs were tied up there for fattening. Then suddenly everything went wrong.

Children and adults who ventured in took to their heels, shaking and stammering, unable to explain clearly what they had felt. They had had the feeling the evil eye of an invisible beast or spirit had bored into them. That an unknown force had shouldered them out and sent them flying onto the tarmac road. That a voice had silently screamed insults and threats in their ears. They started to avoid the place. It was then that three Haitian field-workers, who had found jobs at the nurseries but were probably unaware of all the rumors and scares that were starting to pile up in ominous clouds, broke down the front door of the house and spread out their bedding of rags on the dining room floor. When three days had gone by and they still hadn't shown up for work, Loulou sent an overseer to box their ears. He found them stiff in their rags,

---

[4] A traditional French Caribbean stew of breadfruit and pork.

their black tongues hanging out between their teeth. They had great difficulty finding a gravedigger to bury them as well as a priest to recite the De Profundis.

Moïse therefore supposed that this mahogany tree of a man had met and confronted far more disturbing spirits than those which haunted the Alexis house. The stranger began to speak, spiking each word with a strong foreign accent; Spanish, Moïse said to himself, who had heard Cubans talk in Miami.

"You're the postman, right? I won't waste time beating about the bush. My name is Francisco Alvarez-Sanchez. If you receive letters addressed to that name, they're mine. Otherwise, for every-body here, I'm Francis Sancher. Got it?"

Moïse just missed a stupid hen that was running with its brood right in the middle of the road and dared to exclaim:

"Francisco Alvarez-Sanchez? In which country did you dig that name up?"

"Don't ask questions! The truth might burn your ears!"

Moïse didn't breathe another word.

When they arrived in front of the Alexis house, Francisco, or rather Francis, extracted his huge frame from the van and re-mained standing with all his height examining his property. Then he turned to Moïse and joked:

"It needs a good carpenter, right?"

Moïse got out of the van and the words jostled to get out of his mouth:

"No use, you won't find one. Nobody will agree to work here. But I'll help you! I'll help you!"

People say that on the first night Francis Sancher spent in Rivière au Sel the wind in its temper screamed down from the mountains, trampling the banana plantations and throwing the young yam poles to the ground. Then it jumped on the back of the sea which was peacefully sleeping and lashed it, scarring it with troughs several feet deep.

But people will say anything.

Moïse can confirm that nothing of the sort happened. That night there was not even a breeze. It was as bright as day. The moon was admiring its chubby face in the mirrors of ponds and rivers. The toads, up to their necks in mud, persistently asked for water, over and over again. Moïse was smoking his pipe in his hammock. It was not his desire for a woman that was torturing him, as it did every night. It was those dreams that were taking root again. Around nine o'clock, he could stand it no longer. He jumped to the ground, grabbed a bottle of Montebello rum and set off for the Alexis house.

People began to find the friendship between Moïse and this Francis Sancher, who sprang from God knows where, a bit strange. The first evening the two men stepped into Chez Christian for a shot of rum the locals felt like shoving them out. However, since Francis's shoulders were as wide as a carpenter's bench, they merely whispered slyly behind his back. Some of them said among themselves that they would teach Moïse a lesson. Then they remembered that his family had always been slightly cracked. Sonson, the father, who had pretended to leave for Dominica to fight with the Free French Forces like all the boys of his generation, had, in fact, taken another direction and mooned away his time on another island while his parents lamented him dead or missing. Once the war was over he had returned with Shawn, a Chinese woman, who up to her death had never really known how to speak properly to her neighbors. Valère, the elder brother, had left to work in the oil fields in Venezuela and was never heard of again. Moïse himself had left school, where he was a hard worker, to become a boxer, of all things! Three times a week he would go down to La Pointe to take lessons from a so-called Doudou Sugar Robinson who said he was from Washington, D.C., but everyone knew he was born and bred in Le Moule. After a trip with his manager to Miami, Moïse began to accost every Tom, Dick and Harry and fill their heads with stories about America. A great and wonderful country where blacks laid down the law in the ring. People thought he was about to jump on the next plane and go back there when he passed his driving test and got himself hired at the post office.

Once there, instead of making a niche for himself, he got mixed up with the unions. You could see him marching in line at every demonstration brandishing placards that read: "The Struggle Goes On." Until the day a disciplinary letter called him to order. After that he contented himself with looking after his mother, for his sister Adèle had left home to marry a good-for-nothing who was only attracted to her light skin, and it's true he took great care of Shawn right up until she died.

In the end the inhabitants of Rivière au Sel shrugged their shoulders and watched as the two inseparable new friends climbed up ladders to patch the roof, rounded the bends on the gutters as best they could, cemented the tiles on the veranda, weeded the property and planted a kitchen garden. Tomatoes. Okra. Chives. Hot peppers. For Moïse was right. However hard Francis scoured the surrounding villages showing the color of his money, however much he wore his voice out phoning across the island, he could find nobody, not even an illegal Haitian, to help him repair his property.

In the very beginning, when the house was really uninhabitable and the rats were ensconced in their holes and the bats squeaked in the interstices of the corrugated iron roof, Francis slept at

Moïse's, sucking a pipe with him after sharing the meals Adèle cooked and sent over twice a day, in accordance with the wishes of her late mother.

Once the house had taken shape, although it wasn't much to look at and Marval the carpenter openly laughed at it, it was Moïse who came to sleep over and drink the nights away. Dare we say it? There were some wicked sneers. There was something fishy about that friendship and the two men were makoumeh![5] That's for sure.

Many of the inhabitants in this hardly God-fearing village, buried in the back of beyond, were ignorant of the vices common in towns and had never seen a makoumeh except for Sirop Batterie who dressed up as a woman at carnival time in Petit-Bourg. They inspected the two in disbelief. Moïse, perhaps! But Francis! He didn't look like one. The poisonous plant of mischief, however, grew and flourished in the compost of the village and only wilted once the news of the affair with Mira broke out. Can a rapist of women be a makoumeh as well? Can one have a liking for both men and women? They're still debating the issue at Chez Christian in Rivière au Sel. But what revolted the villagers of Rivière au Sel and set them against Francis was not his dubious relationship with Moïse. Not even that business of rape. It was the fact he did nothing with his ten fingers. Traditionally, the inhabitants of Rivière au Sel worked with wood. In the past, some would set off to attack the giants of the dense forest. They could cut you down and saw you up a candlewood, ironwood or a golden spoon tree in next to no time. Others were excellent builders and could set you up with a timberwork of red cedar. The rest were expert cabinetmakers, who whispered their secrets by word of mouth from father to son and could fashion you mahogany or rosewood chests of draw-

---

[5] *Homosexuals.*

ers, beds made of locust wood and pedestal tables of podocarp
delicately encrusted with magnolia. Those days are long gone, alas,
since Guadeloupe, that cruel stepmother, no longer nurtures her
children, and so many of them are forced to freeze to death in the
Paris suburbs. And yet, wherever they are, the sons of Rivière au
Sel are religious about work. In the dreary workshops or automo-
bile assembly lines where they labor, they remember where they
came from and the respect their parents commanded. What was
Francis doing?

He set up a white deal table on the veranda, placed a typewriter on it and sat down in front of it. When the villagers, who
were intrigued and itching to know what he was doing up there,
stopped Moïse's van they were told he was a writer.

Writer? What's a writer?

The only person they gave that title to was Lucien Evariste,
and that was mainly a joke, because ever since he had returned
from Paris he didn't miss a single opportunity to talk about the
new novel he was working on. Was a writer then a do-nothing,
sitting in the shade on his veranda, staring at the ridge of
mountains for hours on end while the rest sweated it out under the Good Lord's hot sun? And yet Francis Sancher seemed to
have everything he wanted. Every day a truck would rush
through Rivière au Sel delivering him a refrigerator, a TV set or a
stereo. To cap it all, a van bearing the red lettering "MAZUREL
KENNELS—ANIMALS OF ALL KINDS" buzzed through the village one
high noon and delivered the two Dobermans, at the time hardly
bigger than kittens, but already rapacious and greedy for the fresh
blood of innocent creatures, so the neighbors were forced to im-
prison their chickens in their yards. And that's a writer? Come
now!

The most outlandish stories began to circulate. Francis Sancher
was said to have killed a man back in his own country and run off

with his money. They said he was a dealer of hard drugs, one of those the police stationed on Marie-Galante were desperately looking for. An arms runner supplying the guerrillas of Latin America. Since nobody could ever substantiate these accusations, people got carried away. What did prove true was that Francis Sancher's income was of dubious origin.

Moïse paid no attention to the dreadful things people were whispering and did not even take the trouble to tell Francis Sancher. The latter appeared to be unaware of the little esteem he commanded and went on handing out smiles and hellos, left, right and center. You need to have lived inside the four walls of a small community to know its spitefulness and fear of foreigners.

When he went back as far as he could remember and saw himself as a small boy trotting along on his bowlegs hunting butterflies, Moïse could hear the people on the other side of his parents' rayo hedge, who had stopped to look at him, say loud enough for Shawn to hear: "Misbegotten freak! Ta la led pa mechanste!" (That one's really ugly!)

At school the teacher forgot about him, half Chinese, half black, as he daydreamed, so that on the rare occasions she did turn to him he remained speechless, trying to open his eyes wide while the other children snickered. When he could no longer quench the desires of his body, he dropped in on Angelica, a dame-gabrielle,[6] who had landed up in Rivière au Sel at the end of some long tangled career. But she rejected him.

"If I take you what will the others think?"

He had gone home heavy-hearted with rage and regret, and ever since he had lived alone.

---

[6] *A prostitute.*

Yes, that's all he had ever known, the meanness of men's hearts!

But for the time being he had a friend, more than a friend, a child! From the very first weeks of their life together he had realized that Francis Sancher was not at all what he had imagined. Not at all the tree under whose shade he could blossom! His mind was not cut out for the size of his body. Francis Sancher was weak and whining, as scared as a new boy in a turbulent schoolyard, like a newborn arriving in the world of the living. His sleep was not filled with voyages to paradise, but struggles with invisible spirits who, judging from his shouts, stuck their red-hot irons into every corner of his soul. Moïse was not prepared to forget the first night they had slept under the same roof.

He had given him the room looking south with plenty of sunshine where his mother had slept the sleep of a woman alone before passing on as quietly as she had lived. Sonson, his father, had never taken the trouble to explain why he had abruptly left his hotheaded companions off the coast of Roseau, who were going to give de Gaulle a helping hand against the Germans, and had gone on to Jamaica. Had he got scared? Had he realized at the last minute he was going to get shot up in white folks' business? He had never taken the trouble to explain either where and how he had met this ageless Chinese woman who had bequeathed to her three unfortunate children her skinny body, her featureless face and slit eyes, and who was given no more consideration than the furniture in the house right up to the morning he left for work and never came back. Shawn had waited for him a week as silently as ever. Then with dry eyes she went to look for work at the Lameaulnes'. Moïse had grown up amid the smell of their dirty linen that his mother washed at home.

It was past midnight. One or two in the morning. The dogs and the cows had stopped chasing their echoes. The bats were still flitting back and forth, still undecided, worn out as they were, about settling down under the galvanized metal roofs. Suddenly he had heard a shriek that could make your blood curdle, followed by gaspings and groans. He first thought a neighbor had strangely chosen to slit his pig's throat in the middle of the night. Then he had realized that the din was shaking the wall behind the head of his bed and was therefore coming from the next room. He had rushed in and found Francis, a crazed look in his eyes, shouting meaningless phrases:

"One can't lie to one's own flesh and blood! One can't change sides! Swap one role for another. Break the chain of misery. I've tried and you see, nothing's changed. After all, it's only justice. If the sun rose on the other side of the world, lighting first the West then the East, how would the world work? Perhaps it would be like in the fairy tale where the flowers grow roots up, where man's body grows warm only to grow cold and where speech is given to the wisest, in other words the animals? . . . You, do you believe we are born the day we are born? When we land up sticky and blindfolded in the hands of a midwife? I'm telling you we're born well before that. Hardly have we swallowed our first breath of air than we already have to account for every original sin, every sin through deed and omission, every venial and mortal sin committed by men and women who have long returned to dust, but leave their crimes intact within us. I believed I could escape punishment! I couldn't!"

Moïse had had to take him in his arms like the child he would never have and sing him one of those lullabies that Shawn used to sing him in times gone by:

"La ro dan bwa
Ti ni an jupa
Peson pa savé ki sa ki adanye

Sé an zombi kalanda
Ki ka manjé . . ."

(Up there in the woods, there's an ajoupa.[7] Nobody knows who lives there. It's a kalanda zombie who's eating . . .)

In the small hours of the morning, Francis finally went back to sleep, tossing and sweating like a person with the dengue fever. During a quiet moment over coffee Moïse had dared ask:

"Why don't you tell me what's weighing so heavily on your heart? That's what friends are for! To share in the difficulties of this bitch of a life!"

Francis Sancher hadn't opened his mouth. The next day, not in the least discouraged, Moïse had pushed the interrogation further:

"You told me you'd seen some places in your time. Have you been to Africa? They say that over there men and cows lie down to die of the same thirst on the corrugated earth . . . And America? Have you been to America? When I was seventeen I went to Miami with my coach because I wanted to be a boxer. Oh, it's different over there. By kicking and biting, the black folks manage to get to the top of the ladder. Everybody's got a car, you know, that takes them wherever they want to go, docile as a dog . . ."

Francis Sancher had interrupted him roughly:

"Don't talk about what you don't know, man! I've lived in America and I can tell you what goes on there."

Hurt, as when the children used to insult him at school with a "kouni a manman-aw,"[8] Moïse hadn't said another word.

One afternoon, returning to Francis Sancher's, to his surprise he found him in the company of Emile Etienne, known as the Historian. When and where had these two met? Moïse was eaten

---

[7] *A word of Carib origin designating a small thatched hut.*

[8] *An insult to one's mother.*

up by curiosity and was dying to join in the conversation. But the two men ignored him and he had to stick his nose into a week-old copy of *France-Antilles*.

People say it was Mira, Mira Lameaulnes as everyone called her though she had no right to the name, who brought about the quarrel between Francis Sancher and Moïse. They said Moïse had smelled a woman on his friend's underclothes and got jealous. So he kept himself at home at the other end of the village behind the quickset hedge of his bitterness and ended up joining the camp of enemies of the man he had once adored.

But as I said, people will say anything.

The quarrel between Francis Sancher and Moïse had an altogether different cause.

After the visit by Emile Etienne, Francis Sancher began to step up his mysterious wanderings through the woods. He neglected his typewriter, getting up at the crack of dawn when the sun was still shaking itself awake in the sky, setting off to trample the dew and not returning home until the middle of the night, so exhausted you couldn't get a word out of him, his clothes covered in stickweed. What was he looking for? Like a honeybee or a hummingbird that can't make up its mind where to settle. This question haunted Moïse to such an extent that he began to follow him, but never managed to obtain any definite clues.

And that's how he fell victim to the final temptation.

Francis Sancher owned a trunk. A green metal trunk that he had stowed away in the smallest of the two bedrooms and from which he drew everything. Money for meat, bread or cans of Pal for the dogs. The reams of yellow paper, all the same size, for his typewriter. Old clothes. His favorite books, all in Spanish, except for a Saint-John Perse in La Pléiade collection.

Francis Sancher kept the trunk locked, but illogically he kept the key in a candlestick holder at the head of his bed where anybody could lay hands on it.

Once he had opened the trunk, Moïse had had a rush of emotion. Money! Banknotes! More than he had ever seen since deserting Shawn's womb. Not only the familiar, reassuring French notes, but foreign bills, American, green and narrow, all looking alike and, consequently, deceiving and treacherous. How many were there?

He couldn't help thinking of all those nasty stories the inhabitants of Rivière au Sel made up about Francis Sancher, and his confidence wavered as he sniffed a wad, as if its smell could tell him more. Alas! However it's acquired, money has the same dirty smell.

It was then that the rain started to hammer madly on the roof as if it wanted to warn of an impending danger. Almost immediately the floor began to shake and a voice boomed out:

"Well, I got in just in time!"

When Francis Sancher walked in with water streaming down to his shoes, Moïse was nailed to the spot with the wad of notes stuck to his fingers just like Brer Rabbit punished by fate. Francis Sancher looked him up and down with contempt before letting out:

"So that's what you wanted! I was wondering why you clung to me day after day, sucking my blood like a real mosquito. That's what they call you, don't they? So you're just a dirty little thief! If it was money you wanted, why didn't you ask? If you only knew how little it means to me!"

Frantic, his heart crushed by a terrible pain, Moïse stammered out: "It's not . . . It's not what you're thinking!"

Without giving him another look, Francis Sancher hurled: "Get out of here!" and went on mopping up the water.

Moïse had little choice but to obey.

At Chez Christian the men, totally oblivious, were watching a soccer match on the television and chanting "Ma-ra-do-na, Ma-ra-do-na!" Dodose Pélagie, ensconced in a rocking chair on her veranda was reading a copy of *Maisons et Jardins*.

Moïse got back home, his bed still damp from his nocturnal sweats, and, like a defendant too poor to pay for a lawyer, began to prepare his own defense:

"You think I'm after your money. But if it was money I wanted, I would have gone on boxing. I would have become featherweight champion. Doudou Robinson said I had the makings of one. Money's nothing to me. I was looking to find out who you were in order to protect you. Do you understand what I'm saying?"

Those were sad days.

The rain never stopped. The Ravine Vilaine overflowed its banks, swelled and in a flow of blackish silt delivered up the bodies of animals it had caught off guard in the savannas. A terrible stench rose up, and in order to drive it away enormous quantities of incense were burnt in the shrines built into the hillsides.

One evening, unable to stand the pain any longer, Moïse took advantage of a break in the clouds and ran to Francis's, words upon words of explanation in his mouth, his feet going in and out of the mud with greedy sucking noises. Sated, the Dobermans were yawning at the end of their chain.

He was about to push open the gate when the silhouette of a woman appeared on the veranda, the golden mop of hair of a high yellow girl lighting up the evening. Unable to believe his eyes, Moïse recognized Mira and he stood watching her, paralyzed, as if he were seeing her for the first time, as if from one year to the next he hadn't seen her grow and blossom among them like a forbidden plant whose stems, leaves and flowers exuded a poisonous perfume.

What was she doing there?

Shaking from head to foot, he had crouched down in the shadow of an ebony tree until the rain, which had started up again with a vengeance, had soaked him to the bone. He had then run home in a panic as fast as his legs would carry him.

A few days later at Chez Christian the men had talked of rape. Of course he hadn't believed this rape for a single minute. If one person had raped the other, it was surely not the one being talked about. But that wasn't the issue. What mattered was that ever since then his life had resumed its taste of brackish water. The trees of Rivière au Sel had once again tightened their hold around him like the walls of a jail. He would wake up in the night like he used to, sweating with pain and anguish. At the wheel of his van he would risk his neck by leaning out of the window and looking up at the limitless sky that was capping the heads of other men he would never know.

Leave. Yes, but this time in the direction of which American dream?

His colleagues at the post office often got themselves transferred to French France. You would see them on their annual leave, trailing along a blonde, a lake of sadness at the back of their eyes and the bitter swell of exile furrowing the corners of their mouths.

Leave. But if you were to believe Francis Sancher, who had traveled all over the world, there's not a place under the sun that does not have its share of disillusions. Not a single adventure that doesn't end in bitterness. Not a fight that doesn't finish up in failure. So live in Rivière au Sel forever? End one's days as lonely as a male crab in its hole?

Terrified, Moïse looked around him at the circle of praying women, as if every face was an unfamiliar one, from Mademoiselle Léocadie Timothée's, which old age had kneaded, distorted, misshapened and flattened into a nightmare, to Mira's, a radiant obsession of his nights, and Vilma's, still undefined, emerging from adolescence. An unknown pain ripped across his chest and salty water welled up over his eyelids.

Dinah Lameaulnes broke into a new psalm:

"Praise ye the Lord!
Praise ye the Lord from the heavens:
Praise Him in the heights.
Praise ye Him, all his angels!"

He bent his head very low and mingled his voice with the choir of others.

Mira

The time to go down to the Gully is when the sun has set, when the water is black, in places quiet like a dark hole over the black of nothingness, in others running and leaping over rocks, indistinguishable to the naked eye. As a child I used to go down to the Gully at the end of every afternoon and I would stay there for hours on end. I had discovered how good the water tastes at that hour when the night gradually rolls in. I would huddle up under the leaves of the giant philodendron and hear their angry voices:

"Where has she disappeared to again? Why don't they leave her there!"

"That child deserves a good hiding. But her papa won't let anyone lay a finger on her."

When the noise of voices had died down, I would take off my dress and then all my clothes. I would slip into the water that burned from the heat of the day and penetrated to the very depths of my body. I thrilled to this rough fondling. Then I sat on the bank and dried myself with the wind.

The time to go down to the Gully is when the sun has set and the sky is round and hollow like a painted shell above our heads.

Sometimes when I couldn't sleep in the middle of the night I would tiptoe along the corridor that went through the center of the house. On the right I could hear my father snoring; he had not yet married Dinah, the girl from Saint-Martin, and had just finished making love with Julia, our maid. On the left, a ray of light shone from under the door of my brothers' room. One of them, probably Aristide, must have been reading some dirty book. In the garden the dogs ran up to me, whining and wagging their tails. They wanted to follow me, but I chased them away for at night the Gully belonged only to me. I hate the sea, noisy and purple, that tangles your hair. I don't particularly like the rivers, slow-flowing and murky. I only like the gullies, alive, even violent. I bathe there. I sleep on their banks inhabited by batrachians. I twist my ankles on their slippery rocks. This is my realm and mine alone. Ordinary people are afeared, believing the place to be the lair of spirits. So you never meet anyone there. So that when I stumbled on his body, invisible in the dark like a devil's darning needle,[9] I thought here's a man like myself who has come looking for me.

---

[9] Insect common to dark and humid places.

Solitude is my companion. She has cradled and nourished me. She has never left me up to this very day. People talk and talk, but they don't know what it's like to emerge burning hot from the stone-cold womb of your mother, to say farewell to her from the very first moment you enter this world. My father wiped his red eyes. He had loved his black-skinned Rosalie, his Rosalie Sorane with her breasts the color of aubergine.

"Be brave, Monsieur Lameaulnes!" the midwife kept saying.

My father did not have any daughters. His first wife, Aurore Dugazon, who has since died of a fibroma, gave him only boys. Three boys, one after the other. So he took me in his arms and poured his hot tears over my face. But from that moment on I didn't want his love. I didn't want to give him mine. He was guilty.

For if he had left her alone, Rosalie Sorane, if he had let her sleep at her mama's house, her mama who sat five times a week in the market on the rue Hincelin selling tomatoes, okra and green beans and wanted her daughter to go and study at the university in French France, Rosalie Sorane would not have been dead at eighteen, drained of her young blood and lying with cold feet between two embroidered linen sheets.

My father wrapped me in a blue baby's cape, since Rosalie Sorane had wanted a boy and had prepared all her layette in this color, and then laid me in the back of his big American car. When we arrived at Rivière au Sel after an hour's drive, it was dark. A cool wind was blowing down the sides of the mountain, its massive silhouette cut out like a shadow show. Aurore Dugazon, pale and sickly, was sitting on the veranda. My father passed her by without as much as a look, as he always did, and handed me to Minerve, the maid, who had rushed out on hearing the car.

"We'll christen her next Saturday!" was all he said.

The following Saturday I was baptized at the church in Petit-

Bourg: Almira (the name of my grandmother, my father's mother) Rosalie Sorane. Because however much my father was on first-name terms with all the bank directors, the president of the chamber of commerce and the president of the tourist board, he could not change a child born of adultery into a legitimate one. Despite all that, I was never called anything else but Mira Lameaulnes.

At the age of five I ran away for the first time. I could not accept the fact there was no mama somewhere on this earth for me. I was convinced she was hiding in the mountains, she was guarded by the giants of the dense forest and sleeping between the huge toes of their roots. One day when I had been looking for her since morning, I followed a forest path. I was dragging my feet along. Tired to death. Then I stumbled on a rock and tumbled down to the bottom of a gully, hidden under the mass of vegetation. I have never forgotten that first meeting with the water, the scarcely audible babble and the smell of rotting humus.

When they found me after hunting for three days and three nights, my brother Aristide said mockingly:

"Your mama was a Negro wench who took in men. How did you get the idea she's up in the mountains? By now she's probably under our feet roasting in Hell, her skin scorched like pig's crackling."

He could be as spiteful as he liked, however, it didn't bother me. I had found my mother's bed.

Ever since that day, every time my heart is wounded by the spitefulness of the inhabitants of Rivière au Sel, sharpening their knives of malicious words, I go down to the Gully. I go down on the anniversary of Rosalie Sorane's death, which is also my birthday, and I try to imagine what life would be like if she were here watching me grow up, waiting for me on the veranda as I come home from school and explaining to me all the mysteries of a woman's body that I have to discover by myself. It's no use relying on Dinah!

I was very fond of Aurore Dugazon, Aristide's mama, who was so pale, so pale you knew she wouldn't live. When she died they covered all the mirrors with black and purple shawls so that she wouldn't come and look at herself, lamenting her lost youth.

"Good Lord, she looks just like a bride!" people said.

Aristide locked himself up in his room. It was my father who went to fetch him and threatened to beat him if he didn't come and give her a last kiss before the coffin was nailed down.

I thought he was going to die too that day! That's why we were both ready for Dinah, the second wife, when she turned up one morning from Saint-Martin. Aristide had warned me:

"You'll see how I'm going to teach her her place."

But he didn't have to. It wasn't us who taught her her place.

At first Dinah blossomed like a lily. In the morning she would sing in front of her window which would be opened wide to let in the cool air from the mountains. She had the entire house scrubbed with vetiver and bundles of leaves. The air was heavy with perfume. In the evening she would tell us stories.

Soon, alas, we saw her languish and wilt like grass deprived of morning dew. My father no longer spoke to her. He passed her by without as much as a glance. At table he would push his plate away after the first mouthful. In the evening he went out or else locked himself up in one of the bedrooms in the attic with a woman he'd picked up God knows where, and we could hear them laugh and laugh behind the closed door. Whenever my eyes met his he would sneer:

"If looks could kill."

It was true I was suffocating with hatred and wondering what I could think up to hurt him. That's why I let myself be influenced by Aristide. In actual fact I loved him only like a brother. But I thought I had found my happiness in this taste for evil and forbidden fruit.

Very soon, even that was no longer enough. Ever since I had been expelled from my fourth paying school, I did nothing but shoot up joylessly like a plant going to seed. I started to have a dream, always the same dream, night after night. I was shut up in a house without doors or windows and I was trying to get out, but couldn't. Suddenly someone knocked on a wall that cracked and crumbled and I came face to face with a stranger, as solid as a tree, who rescued me.

I killed time during the day as best I could. At one point, Aristide got it into his head to find me work at the nurseries. I would arrange bouquets for the brides and wreaths for the dead. But all the men could do while I was there was devour me with their lecherous eyes. So that didn't last very long. Sometimes my father would look at me and say:

"I'll have to find you a husband! When I've got time for you."

I didn't even bother to answer.

Life began when I went down to the Gully. One evening, very much like any other, when the air was full of fireflies just like any other, I set off down the familiar path. I was about to go near the water when I stumbled on his body hidden by the philodendron leaves. He sat up and asked:

"Is it you? Is it you?"

I shone my flashlight on his face in the dark. I recognized him at once.

"Were you waiting for me?" I whispered.

"I didn't expect you so soon," he stammered.

I bent over him:

"You think it's too soon? Me, I've been waiting for you for

twenty-five years and nothing ever happened. I was going to give up."

"Twenty-five years? How come twenty-five years?" he asked.

I laid my hand on his shoulder. He was shaking all over.

"What are you afraid of?" I asked.

"Of you of course. How will you do it?"

I got right up close and pressed my mouth against his, dry, lifeless and unresponsive.

"Like that!"

After that kiss he stared at me with eyes crazed with incomprehensible terror.

"Is that all?"

I laughed.

"No! Let's go on if you want."

I unbuttoned his dark blue shirt, undid his stiff leather belt. He didn't say a word. He was like a child with a grown-up. We made love on the bed of leaves at the foot of the giant tree ferns. He succumbed, without resistance, but watched my every movement as if he thought I would deal him some fatal blow. Then he lay motionless a long while beside me and finally he said:

"My name is Francis Sancher."

"I know that, silly," I answered.

He turned towards me.

"You're not the one I've been waiting for. Who are you?"

I got up and went down towards the water that sparkled black between the rocks.

"I'm surprised you don't know who I am," I laughed. "The people from Rivière au Sel tell all sorts of stories about me."

"They run from me like the plague. Nobody speaks to me."

"Not even Mosquito?"

"Mosquito?"

I ran the water over my hair.

"Moïse, if you prefer. That's how they call your friend the postman. Hasn't he mentioned me?"

He didn't reply.

In the dark I could hear the heavy tread of the toads as they hunted insects under the leaves. Suddenly, the wind felt icy on my shoulders and I got out of the water to put on my clothes. He continued to watch me in silence. As I was leaving, he asked:

"Will I see you again?"

"Looks as though you've taken a liking to it!" I called out over my shoulder.

The people of Rivière au Sel don't like me. The women pray to the Holy Mother when they pass me by. The men recall their nocturnal dreams when they soaked their sheets and they're ashamed. So they defy me with their eyes to hide their desire.

Why? Probably because I'm too beautiful for their ugliness, too light-complexioned for the blackness of their hearts and skins. Despite appearances my father is afraid of me. He can badger his overseers and his Haitian workers. He can rule with an iron hand his children from his second marriage, not to mention Dinah, his very own zombie. He can dismiss the maids at the snap of his fingers, when he is tired of them or when they stand up to him. With me, it's different. He knows the body of Rosalie Sorane is between us. Aristide too is afraid of me, of my moods, my fits as he calls them. When I arrived in Rivière au Sel, wrapped in my blue baby's cape, Aristide had just turned three. He let go of his mother's hand for me. We grew up like two savages. We know each other's secrets. But I have never taken him down to the Gully. That place is mine. It's my realm and my refuge.

Aristide says he could never live far from the mountains. Every morning he delves deep into their belly and returns with his backpack full of yellow-footed thrushes, black woodpeckers, partridges and woodpigeons that he has limed among the ferns and that he keeps in bamboo cages at the bottom of the nurseries. His realm is his greenhouse of orchids. Those people who say his heart is as hard as stone don't know him. His heart is as tender as a little child's.

The day I met Francis Sancher down in the Gully I came across Aristide smoking on the veranda.

"Where have you been hanging around again?" he growled.

I showed him my back and went up to my room. He followed me and plopped himself down in the rocking chair. I started arranging my hair for the night. Then I began my questions, being careful with my intonation as I knew how jealous he could be.

"What are people saying about Francis Sancher?"

His eyes burnt right through me.

"Why, are you interested in him?"

"Isn't everyone interested in him round here?"

"People say he's a Cuban. When Fidel opened the doors of his country, he left."

"Why did he come here, where there's no work and nothing to do?"

"That's the question!"

There was silence. Then he went on:

"Listen, I'm going to tell you a story.

"One Sunday at Mass, Ti-Marie saw a man she hadn't seen before, all dressed in white, wearing a Panama hat. On leaving the church she asked her godmother: 'Godmother, oh Godmother, did you see that handsome man in a Panama hat? Do you know his name?' "

I shrugged my shoulders.

"Stop your silly stories! What do you think I am, a baby?"

He got up and went out without saying a word.

Night is not made for sticking in bed like a cartwheel stuck in the mud of a cane field. Night is made for dreaming wide-awake. It is made for reliving the sparse moments of happiness that make up the day. I relived the moments I spent with Francis Sancher. Up till then, I had caressed only one familiar body, that held no mystery and was as close to mine as the trunk of the candlewood is to the epiphytical philodendron. Now I had to discover what lay behind this unfamiliar physique. Like Ti-Marie, in love at first sight with the stranger in the Panama hat, all dressed in white, I had to find out who he was.

At breakfast my father was fidgeting impatiently like an unruly horse. He started on Joby, the eldest of his children from his second marriage, a sickly boy who was scared of everything.

"Why do I spend my money sending you to school, eh? You're no better than those Haitian niggers carting manure in my nurseries."

For once Dinah protested:

"Remember he was sick with the dengue fever up until yesterday."

He pounced on her.

"Shut your mouth when I'm talking to my children!"

Then he turned to Aristide.

"What do you mean by clearing the savanna, in Heaven's name?"

Aristide did not lose his calm and went on quietly to finish his coffee.

"I went to Martinique and visited the Balata gardens. Some guy had the idea of growing all sorts of flowers and plants in his grandmother's 'change of air' property. The tourists come from all over and pay admission. Why not us? We've got acres of land and just the right climate."

"Except that tourists never come round here!" he sneered.

"They'll come if there's something to see!"

I knew they were going to start bickering and to go for each other like dogs, so I went out onto the veranda. Morning is my favorite time of day. The leaves are dancing gently on the trees freshly woken by the sun. The air smells of water.

Curled up in the rocking chair where Dinah cultivates her solitude from six in the evening onwards, I saw Mosquito hand over the post to Cornélia.

If ever anybody followed and spied on me with his slit eyes, it was Mosquito. One day I was walking along the ridge at Dillon, where you can see the clouds scampering over the sea, when I met him wandering like a lost soul. He smiled at me.

"Hello, sweetie! Can I walk along the road with you a little way?"

I did not even take the trouble to reply. He stood fidgeting for a moment and then went off with his tail between his legs.

That morning, however, he seemed a godsend and I ran out to him.

"Take me to the shop. I want to see if they have any writing paper."

I wasn't too sure how to get the conversation on to Francis Sancher, when I noticed a letter in the basket where he kept the bundles of mail tied up with different-colored elastic bands. It had a rare and unusual name, Francisco Alvarez-Sanchez, so different from those in Rivière au Sel who were called Apollon, Saturne, Mercure, Boisfer, and Boisgris. The masters really had fun baptizing their slaves!

I realized immediately who it was, but I acted innocent.

"Does he live in Rivière au Sel?"

"Put my letter down!" he shouted. "Don't you know you could go to jail for that if you were in America!"

What does he know about America? Aristide went to America once. For an orchid exhibition in Monterey. He told me about the white birds and the trees carved by the wind.

I laid my hand on his knee, hard and pointed like a pebble from the river, and he began to tremble so much that I took pity on this ugly body that would never know what love is.

"What do you know about him?"

He attempted a laugh, but his eyes were gleaming like an animal's.

"What will you give me if I tell you what I know? A kiss?"

I didn't bother to answer.

"His family comes from here and he's trying to trace them," he stammered. "They were white Creoles who fled after abolition."

"Is that all?" I looked him up and down. "Look, Moïse, if you want your kiss, you'd better find out something better than that."

And thereupon I got out of his van and slammed the door. People were already staring at us.

I waited a week, two weeks, but Mosquito never came to see me. I went down to the Gully every night, but Francis Sancher never came back.

Back home, I sent Aristide away. He didn't understand what was going on and I moistened my pillow with tears of salt.

Love, like death, takes you by surprise. It does not march in beating the gwo-ka.[10] Its foot slowly sinks into the soft earth of the heart. Suddenly I lost my sleep, I lost the inclination to drink and eat. All I could think about was the time spent in the Gully,

---

[10] A traditional drum from Guadeloupe.

which apparently was never to be relived since he had forgotten me.

It was a Monday. I remember it was Monday because my father went down to La Pointe once a week and lunched with his cousin Edgar the cardiologist, whom he can't stand. The night unlocked the door to the wind outside. You should always beware of the wind outside, beware of its demented voice that booms and bounces across hills and savannas, that creeps into every nook and cranny and sows chaos, even in the closed calabashes of our heads. It was the wind that got it into my head. There I was, lying on my bed, when it began to whirl around me, pestering me:

"Go on! Go on! Go to him! Don't sit there crying your eyes out!"

I had just got back from the deserted Gully whose waters had wrapped themselves round my spurned body like a shroud. Why had he said: "Will I see you again?" if he didn't know the meaning of these words? If he didn't know he was setting up another meeting?

All the way back, the oblong moon had bobbed in front of me, laughing at my grief:

"Mira, Mira Lemeaulnes, what's come over you? You're nothing but a rag doll crying for a man."

Now that I know the end of the story, my story, and I ended up like Ti-Marie being eaten alive, I can't understand why I placed all my hopes in this man whom I didn't know from Adam. Probably because he came from Elsewhere. From over there. From the other side of the water. He wasn't born on our island of malice that has been left to the hurricanes and the ravages caused by the spitefulness in the hearts of black folks.

From Elsewhere.

Yes, it was the wind outside that planted this idea in my head under the sweltering heat of my hair. A crazy, senseless idea since

I was going to give my life and my love to someone who was waiting for death.

At the crack of dawn I threw everything that came to hand into a wickerwork basket. And then I went out. The wind outside had died down. The water from the rain flattened the tall bright green grass as it washed it afresh. Everything seemed to be waiting for the sun to make up its mind. For a moment I got scared. I saw myself as a mad woman wearing a dress of leaves, setting off along the road to misfortune. I almost turned back. But then I remembered the miserable life I was leaving back there, and my longing to live, at last, in the sun got the better of me. I set off down the road.

Aristide

"That's not how he should have died. His blood, his blood should have been made to flow and avenge my sister."

With these thoughts stuck in his head like a murderous fragment of flint, Aristide entered the house. Until now he had kept his distance from this corpse whom he continued to hate, even though it was but a corpse. But the rain had begun to drum on the green tarpaulin and leaked down through a

Z-shaped tear, lapping in a pool of mud at the feet of the rum drinkers. At each gust of wind it also flooded the veranda and soaked the gossipers. From the dining room, where he was obliged to take refuge amid the smell of sweat, flowers and melted candles, he could see the funeral bed and part of the circle of women. Mira was kneeling on her two knees, lost in prayer. He would have liked to pull her by the hair, slap her and beat her as he had done when they were children, reminding her of all the shame this man had brought on her name and on their family. Despite the fiery taste of the rum he had swallowed, shot after shot, his throat felt dry and rough.

The day when Mira had left the house to go and live with this criminal, little suspecting what lay in store, he had risen as usual in the dark and taken off for the mountains. He knew every track, every path up there. He had followed his favorite path, the Saint-Charles, that starts at Bois Sergent, loses itself in the rain forest and ends up against the crater of the Soufrière amid its damp and purple steam.

Only there, among the giant trees, the marbri, châtaignier, candlewood, mastwood and Caribbean pines, did he feel at home. He would slip into their serene and silent shadows, broken here and there by the twittering of birds. In the days when his father used to speak to him, before jealousy and hatred poisoned the air between them, his father would tell of the times gone by when the rough hand of man had not yet ravished the forests of Guadeloupe and they were teeming with all sorts of birds. Macaws with breasts as red as embers, hornbills with beaks and eyes painted in crimson, fluffy green-and-red parakeets, and parrots that could easily be taught to speak. His father would turn the pages of *Nouveau Voyage aux Isles de l'Amérique*[11] and he watched with a child's

---

[11] *By Père Labat.*

fascination as the plates appeared one after the other in a soft rustling of paper.

It made him dream. What had his island looked like before it had been auctioned off through the greed and love of lucre of the settlers? Like the Paradise his catechism described. Yes, it was Loulou who had instilled in him this love of trees and birds. Now, alas, the forest was a desecrated cathedral. You had to be content with paltry takings . . .

His gamebag heavy with woodpigeons that he had caught too easily, he made a detour by way of the Waterfall des Ecrevisses. A horde of Canadian tourists, who were dabbling their pale feet amid shrieks of laughter, made him retreat. When he got home around nine in the morning, Dinah was waiting for him on the veranda.

"She's gone!"

He shrugged his shoulders.

"It's not the first time she's disappeared. She's stayed out all day and all night before, hasn't she?"

Dinah looked up with watery eyes.

"But it's not the same! Have you ever seen her take her things with her? Her shoes, her dresses, her bras . . . ?"

Unmoved, he turned his back and went off to cuss the Haitian workers who thought they could earn their money doing nothing. He did regret, however, not having badgered her the day before to find out what she was hiding under her mop of hair. Nevertheless, he wasn't really worried. She was probably twisting her ankles on the rocks of some ravine like a young goat. Once she got tired of living off rose apples and governor plums, she would find her way back home. The next morning he didn't think too much about it. Nor the morning after that.

It was nightfall when Moïse the postman burst into the dining room where the family was swallowing the thick evening soup in silence and the children were being careful not to make their usual slurping noises, since they could sense their father's fury and their mother's anxiety.

"She's at his place! His place!" he shouted.

"Whose place?" Dinah had asked stupidly. "Who are you talking about?"

Aristide, for one, had already understood. In fact, he had briefly sensed something that evening she had asked him in an unconvincing voice what he knew about Francis Sancher. He was wrong to have let his suspicions be lulled.

However crazy and capricious she was, Mira was lovely and light-skinned enough to catch a husband. Dr. Jouvenel was not the only one to come up from La Pointe and request her hand for his third son, who had studied in Canada.

"I'm not unduly concerned about her behavior! It's her age. Once a man has stuck his rod in the right place she'll be as soft as a glove."

Mira shook her head each time she was consulted. She did not want a man at her side. So Loulou would reply that his daughter was too young. The people of Rivière au Sel got a laugh out of that. Too young! Couldn't he see the two breasts that were pushing hard against her blouse? Somebody was already fondling those fruits, that's for sure, because you don't really think she goes down to the Gully to look at herself in the water!

On that point, Aristide had no worries. Mira's heart belonged to nobody. It was made of that elusive, intractable substance that escapes any form of imprisonment.

Like everyone else, Aristide couldn't stand Moïse and had persecuted him ever since they had been at school. He had gone into a rage when Mira had confided in him that this half pint of a man had dared devour her with his eyes and follow her back from school. He had lain in wait for him, therefore, and surprised him one afternoon while he was bathing in the river Moustique dressed in a ridiculous pair of flowery undershorts. He had threatened to wring his cock's neck and then went on to give him a good thrashing.

Apparently Moïse had not held it against him since he had come to warn the family of its misfortune!

Loulou was already up and shouting:

"Let's go! What are you waiting for, for God's sake!"

When they arrived at Francis's with Moïse trailing behind, Francis Sancher was at table and Mira was fussing around him like a servant.

Appalled, Aristide looked at the room. Was that where she had decided to live? A table, a few whitewood chairs. A black and white television set placed on a stool that made Monique, the star-announcer, lose all the effect of her eye makeup. On the floor, a fan grated, fighting against the humidity.

Despite the resolutions he had repeatedly made to himself on the way there, rage drowned Aristide's reason. Words had not seemed adequate and he had thrown himself on Francis, set on bloodying his handsome, impudent face. He had, however, underestimated his opponent. Nothing in common with the niggers he sent flying to the edge of the cane fields with his fist. Francis Sancher had rammed his ribs with kicks, gripped him viciously by the neck and left him panting and gasping for air in the dust. Humiliation of humiliations, it was Moïse who ran to fetch him a beaker of water.

Once calm had been somewhat restored, Francis Sancher hammered out:

"I did not ask her to come here. She came of her own accord. I am not keeping her. In fact, ever since she arrived I've been asking her to return home."

Loulou had begun to shout, but it was obvious he was utterly helpless.

"Nonsense! You'll pay for this, you scoundrel!"

Francis had burst out laughing.

"Pay for what? What do you want me to pay for?"

There was silence during which they could hear the frantic barking of the dogs. Then Francis went on:

"I was not the first, if you want to know. You haven't looked after your daughter. Another man has already made a wide passage."

Involuntarily, Loulou turned to Aristide, who reeled under his look. Suspecting nothing, Francis Sancher went on mockingly:

"And I didn't have to ask. She propositioned me herself. Why don't you tell them, Mira?"

Mira had looked up and her eyes were full of tears.

"He's telling the truth," she said quietly. "He was not the first one."

"You're lying! You're lying!"

Who had shouted that? Aristide had no idea.

Once again, fury heaved him up in her black swell. Once again, he threw himself on Francis Sancher, bit the dust and looked up with a bloodied face at the small crowd who were counting the blows.

Those who attended the wake of Francis Sancher recalled that at eleven-seven precisely, the house began to sway, roll and crack in all its joints while a rumbling shook the air. The pregnant women put their hands to their wombs where the frightened fetuses were kicking. The old folks thought their last hour had come and their entire life spun through their heads. Two days later, which was a Monday, however hard the headlines of *France-Antilles* screamed from town to town: "EARTHQUAKE IN GUADE-LOUPE. The tremor was especially strong in the region of Petit-Bourg, Basse-Terre . . ." the inhabitants of Rivière au Sel didn't believe a word, and remained convinced that it was Francis Sancher who had played a last trick on them before shooting off to lose himself in eternity.

Locked in the jail of his thoughts, Aristide did not even feel the tremor, and everyone was amazed at his calm that so contrasted with the general chaos around him.

Back home after that disastrous meeting with Francis Sancher, he had drowned his shame and his pain in straight, white rum, then gone to find Loulou, who was slumped in the armchair in his office.

"We'll prosecute for rape!"

Loulou looked up with two sparkling eyes and thundered:

"Rape? What rape? Don't give me that bullshit!"

But Aristide insisted.

"I'm going down to the police station in Petit-Bourg to file a complaint."

Because the head of police, Ro-Ro, had been a close school comrade, promoted to the rank of chief under his real name Romuald Romulus, Aristide was counting on his support. In his office, where a fly-specked photo of the President of the Republic hung, Ro-Ro was making life difficult for a Rastaman who looked perfectly innocent under his dreadlocks.

"You're wasting your time with this nonsense, while any Tom, Dick and Harry can come and settle in the country . . . ?"

Already informed by public rumor of the Lameaulnes' misfortune, Ro-Ro had the Rastaman taken out and stared at Aristide pityingly.

"You're up bright and early. What can I do for you?"

"I want you to lock up the Cuban for rape and keep him behind bars for a long, long time. That's what I want!"

"Rape?" Ro-Ro had asked. "But where is Mira to make a statement?"

Aristide brought his fist down on the desk.

"You don't need Mira. Because I'm telling you what happened!"

Ro-Ro shook his head and declared in a very administrative tone of voice:

"To convict a person of rape is a very serious business. Especially . . ."

Thereupon he stopped.

"Especially what?" Aristide had broken in. "What do you mean? Say it, so that I can punch you in the mouth!"

Ro-Ro got up and shrugged his shoulders.

"I'm not afraid of you, you know! Listen to me! Some time or another she was going to live her own life. You and your father never found anybody good enough for her and you watched over her like two mongooses over a hen. Perhaps she'll be happy with this man."

Aristide had headed for the door so that he wouldn't have to hear any more of this rubbish.

Outside, the sun shone indifferently and flooded the town's freshly tarred little streets. Two children were standing wide-eyed in front of the window of The Thousand and One Nights, the new shop belonging to a Lebanese.

Aristide headed for Isaure's as fast as he could. In times gone by, when he was less wrapped up in his rather particular brand of love, Aristide had been a frequent visitor to Isaure's, a vivacious câpresse[12] who had passed forty with hardly a wrinkle, and took in men in the low house her parents had left her behind the municipal stadium, so that her lovers brought her to a climax against a background of shouts and bravos from a crowd gone wild. Thank the Lord, people said, that her devout mother, who had been the founder of the Eldest Daughters of the Virgin Mary, was no longer on this earth to see this. At one point, Isaure had been the lead singer in the Paroka group that sang Creole mazurkas and béguines. But the zouk music of those wretched Kassav[13] had done away with all that and Isaure had reverted to amorous dealings.

She received Aristide in her bedroom on the red mahogany bed where she had been born, that was wedged between gueridons, low tables, a wardrobe with a mirror and rocking chairs in the same wood. Practically the only time she got up was to go to Mass on Sundays, for however far she had fallen she still kept her religion.

Already alerted by public rumor, she too pretended to be politely surprised.

"You'd disappeared! Did you wake up dreaming of me this morning?"

Aristide didn't even bother to answer and roughly made room for himself beside her. He had no intention, however, of making love to her, and Isaure felt quite sad, almost watery-eyed, when she recalled the time he used to impale her on his stake.

"I'd like to kill him!" Aristide had groaned. "But then I'm the one they'd throw into jail. And they call this a civilized country!"

---

[12] One of the many French Caribbean color categories: a light-skinned person, usually with a fine head of hair.

[13] An internationally-known band from Guadeloupe.

"You know," Isaure said hesitatingly, "I know that guy and he's not as bad as you think!"

Aristide jumped up.

"He's raped my sister and you're telling me he's not bad!"

Raped! Raped! The guy who could rape Mira Lameaulnes had not yet solidified from his father's sperm, that's for sure. But Isaure kept this thought to herself and Aristide had asked:

"How did you meet him?"

"One day he came in here. I don't know who had told him about me. He must have liked what he found because he came back several times."

"What did he say to you?"

Isaure made a face.

"I didn't listen too much to what he said because I like to sleep afterwards. I used to let him rattle on. He needed affection like a child."

"Spare me, woman. I'm asking you what he said."

"He said he had spent time in Africa where he was a doctor . . ."

"A doctor! That's rubbish!"

"That's what he told me!"

Aristide had left in a panic, almost killing himself a hundred times on the winding road that was slippery from the constant humidity.

How many weeks then dragged on in red, red rage, suffering and pain?

Aristide couldn't stay still for one minute; he would stand up, walk about in a daze and insult people at the slightest pretext. He shunned the mountains. The birds in his aviary twittered miserably to death. He no longer set foot in his greenhouses and brushed aside his gardeners who wanted him to admire some phalaenopsis or smell the scent of the epidendrum mutelianum.

Since he was no longer on their backs at every hour of the day and night, the Haitian workers spent their time glued to the transistor radio, trying to understand the events surrounding the return to democracy in their country.

Manigat?[14] Why not?

Some of them, whose only concern was that Manigat had the right-color skin, were already planning their return home and saw themselves carried along by the crowds down Lalue.[15] Others kept a cool head, having got their fingers burnt so many times before. As for Aristide, he wore out his nights and days asking himself what he could do. What could he invent now that the idea of rape had not taken root?

At three thousand feet the forest of Guadeloupe becomes stunted. Gone are the châtaigniers, the mastwoods, the mountain immortelles and the red cedars. It's the realm of the camasey, its leaves embossed in greenish black, that scarcely grows more than six feet above the ground. The earth becomes a mass of purple-flowered, scentless bromeliads and white orchids streaked with cardinal-colored venules.

Stretched out on this carpet of flowers, Aristide was staring at the impervious hard blue sky as if to defy it and convey his anger. He would have liked to be a stone in a catapult so he could put a hole through its forehead. A man had robbed him of his sister, the treasure of his heart, and this man was allowed to go free, breathing and coming and going as he pleased. And he had not laid him to rest in his final resting place.

At that moment a shadow fell across his face and a foot tram-

---

[14] A brief contender for political power in Haiti.

[15] An avenue in Port-au-Prince.

pled the grass level with his head. He leaped up and saw Xantippe holding a cutlass.

"Sa ou fè?" (Hi!) he grumbled.

But Xantippe as usual had not answered and quickly walked away. In the beginning, the children had been afraid of Xantippe. Pregnant women would protect their fetus with a prayer to the Virgin Mary when they met him. Whenever a hen disappeared from the yard or a spotted calf wandered from its mother's side, people would hold him responsible. Gradually, they grew to realize that he was just a poor devil a bit touched in the head. The know-it-alls swore that he once lived in Capesterre Belle Eau and that he had lost his wits one Christmas Day when, as a gift from the Good Lord, his concubine and four children had been burnt to death when their hovel went up in flames. The next day he could be seen running naked under the sun. When the gendarmes chased him, he took refuge in the woods. Four long years went by before they saw him reappear on a plot of ground that used to belong to the Marquisat factory before it closed its doors, throwing valiant heads of families onto the street. Nobody knew why he had turned up in Rivière au Sel one morning out of the blue.

Aristide looked to see how high the sun was and decided to take the path back to the village. He stopped at Chez Christian. As he entered, the noisy flow of meaningless words dried up. Aristide, who had always despised these men because of the color of their skin and because they owed their survival to his father's nurseries, felt his heart run warm when he looked at their familiar faces. He answered positively to the chorus of "Sa ou fè?" and seized the bottle that Christian was mercifully handing him without further ado. When he left, the trees were dancing on their stilts. The ragged hills were fluttering and jumping over the pale body of the moon sprawled on its fluffy bed.

Dinah was waiting for him on the veranda, rubbing her hands together.

"She's come home!"

He looked at her, uncomprehending.

"She's come home!" she repeated.

Nobody knows exactly what substance the human heart is made of. It endures and endures and then one morning, it's over.

"I've had enough," it declares. "I can't take any more!"

It was when Mira returned home and Aristide saw her soiled, sullied and cast out by a man, that his love abandoned him. He had carried this love for such a long time, perhaps ever since the day she had arrived, wrapped in her blue baby's cape when he himself was still sucking Aurore Dugazon's breast, ever since their games in the savanna hunting hogplums, their childhood cuts and grazes and their teenage moods, so that her sudden disappearance had made him stumble and lose his balance, clutching his deserted chest. At night he would wake to the roar of the wind outside and wonder:

"Is it true then that I don't love her anymore? Can this be possible?"

He caught himself looking at other women, freed of the weight of this guilty love, surprised at the violent reaction of his blood.

One morning, no duller, no more desolate than any other morning in Rivière au Sel, he had been studying some creamy white cattleyas that had freshly bloomed in the warmth of their greenhouse, when suddenly his life had unfolded in front of his eyes—flat and featureless, like the island of Marie-Galante. He was twenty-eight, an age when some men tense their muscles to prove who they are. What had he done? Nothing, except sap a body that was close to his. He had been overcome with self-disgust and turned his head to the sea as if its salt could purify him. He had spent only very brief periods away from the island and was always in a hurry to return home to his lovenest. He had never given a thought to what was happening beyond the horizon, on the other side of the world, and suddenly there was this pressing desire inside him, like that for a woman. From that day onwards it had not let him alone. It was constantly upon him and it drained him of his strength.

Leave, like his two brothers before him, who had quickly tired of Loulou's cussing and kicking and made a life for themselves, one in French France and the other in La Pointe.

Leave. Oh, it wouldn't be easy. He would ask Loulou for the rewards of so many years' hard work and if the old miser wasn't prepared to hear of it, he would use threats.

Yes, he would leave this island without a future where, except for the size of his penis, nothing tells a man he's a man. Flowers have no motherland. They'll perfume any land. So, to America? To Europe? The immense possibilities open to him made him feel dizzy. In fact, perhaps he should be grateful to Francis Sancher for having given him his freedom, for having delivered him from Mira.

He watched her, slumped against Moïse's shoulder like a bride dressed in black, and paradoxically, the sight of this grief caused by another man rekindled his rage and took on the color of wounded love. He recalled all those kisses, all those embraces, the secrecy, the passion, their father's jealousy, and he wondered what would fill his life now.

What master plan? Failing that, what other love?

He changed places and found himself in the middle of a group of men who were guffawing in the heat of alcohol. While Cyrille the storyteller was waiting for the atmosphere to warm up,

Jerbaud, a master joker, was telling one of his tall stories. Aristide felt like driving out all these chatterboxes, these parasites, these drunkards. Death is a serious business, for God's sake! Why keep on with these antics that were fine for the age of Nan-Guinen,[16] but not for today?

While these thoughts were crossing his mind he moved over to the large table and helped himself again to the rum. The liquid exploded in his head and slowly burned down through his body to his feet, imparting an impulse to set them moving, beating time and dancing which, in a way, did not surprise him. After all, wasn't he off to begin his real life?

---

[16] *The time of slavery.*

Mama Sonson

I've lived here now in Rivière au Sel for sixty-three years. It's here I was born. It's here I shall end my days. But it's not here I shall be laid to rest, because there's no graveyard in Rivière au Sel. You have to go and rest in peace at the cemetery in Petit-Bourg among strangers, men and women you don't know from Adam and who died from God knows what.

I would like to be buried right here behind the wooden cabin that Siméon, my late husband, put up with his own two hands; a staunch nigger he was, the likes of which have disappeared from the surface of the earth and you won't find his sort again, however hard you look; I'd like it to be under the grafted mango tree that I planted one September morning, when the moon was on the rise, in this place that I've never left, even when my second son, Robert, got married over there in France to a white woman he met in the post office where he works. A white woman! I cried all the tears out of my body. We're not any old sort of nigger, you know. The white man's eyes have never burned us out. Siméon, my late husband, used to tell how, shortly after abolition, his grandfather Léopold had been whipped to death by a white man for not giving way to him. The region was up in arms about it and Léopold's friends had wanted to avenge him. There was bloodshed. There were deaths. The cane fields had gone up in smoke that climbed high into the sky. A white woman in our family!

I told him:

"Thank goodness your papa's no longer on this earth to see that! The whites put us in slavery. The whites put us in shackles. And you go and marry a white woman!"

He laughed.

"Maman, all that about slavery and shackles, that's ancient history. You've got to live with your times."

Perhaps he's right. Perhaps we should weed out from our heads the Guinea grass and quitch grass of our old grudges. Perhaps we should teach our hearts a new beat. Perhaps those words, black and white, no longer mean anything! That's what I tell myself as I sit rocking back and forth, warming my heart with a drop of rum mixed with honey.

Look at them all around me!

They're pretending to pray to the Good Lord for the unfortunate Francis Sancher and putting on funeral faces as if grief was stifling them.

Yet if I drew up a list for you of all those who trod my floor to ask me to do him harm or even rid the earth of his being, you wouldn't believe me!

I know that not one ray of goodwill ever shines on the heart of niggers. Even so! What could they have against Francis Sancher, who had a heart of gold?

There were those who couldn't stand the din his dogs made when they scoured the night, sinking their fangs into soft, defenseless flesh. There were those who couldn't stand to see him sit and drink rum and the wind on his veranda while they themselves sweated it out under the Good Lord's hot sun. And then there were those who had never forgiven him for taking Mira whom they had lusted after for years. The women were the worst. They hated Mira like salt hates water. To tell the truth, they were jealous of her and unrelenting.

"Who does she think she is? Yes, who does she think she is? Is she forgetting she came out of a woman's belly as black as you and me? Is she forgetting she's a bastard child as well?"

In the secret of my heart I took pity on Mira because I saw misfortune hovering over her. A black cloud over her head. It's not fair skin that is the key to happiness!

Maman, in her time, saw things. She saw the hurricane of 1928. One morning, day broke, black with anger, with wrinkles on its brow.

"Dear, oh, dear! Guadeloupe's in for it today!" she said.

She foresaw the Second World War and that two of her own sons would meet their death in a far-off land. She saw the great fire in La Pointe when the flames in their anger started with the Rialto cinema and only calmed down once they had devoured all the houses of the Carénage district. As a child, thank goodness, I didn't have that gift. My eyes could only see the visible, the familiar. The hopscotch drawn in chalk in the schoolyard, the marbles my brothers used to roll on the sand, and the ragged pages of the storybooks I used to read in the evening. You see, I wasn't a good pupil. I didn't like school, where the mistresses ignored me and coddled the teacher's pet, who brought them bunches of flowers, freshly laid eggs and cuddly white rabbits. But I loved to read! Read! My only regret was that the books never talked about who I was, me, a little black-skinned girl, born in Rivière au Sel. So I made up and imagined my stories in the back of my head. It was only after I had met Siméon, once we were married in church, me in a veil and crown, him in a black suit, that I finished with all that. My children replaced my dreams.

Yes, to start off with, I was spared.

Then one night, right in the very middle, Siméon was sleeping beside me after having given me what he gave me every evening, when something woke me up. Eyes wide open in the dark, I saw as plain as I can see the bed over there surrounded with candles and the picture of Our Lord Jesus Christ that Rosa must have brought because there was nothing that speaks of religion in this house. I saw my oldest brother, Samuel, who was all my mother had left and the apple of her eye, lying in his blood between the roots of a tree. Two days later he was to kill himself as he climbed to pole down a breadfruit for his lunch pot.

That's how it all began!

Ever since that moment, I haven't had a minute's peace from all the suffering, accidents, and deaths. Sometimes I shut my eyes ever so tight, so as not to see any more. But tomorrow is implacable and insists on showing me what it will bring, mercifully hiding it from the eyes of other humans. People think I can ward off all this suffering. Alas! I can but try with the help of God. That's what I'm fighting for and that's why my hair has turned gray before its time from all this weariness. Ever since I turned forty, and even before, I have worn this wig of steel wool that the comb's teeth have a tough time getting through.

I liked Francis Sancher, I'm not afraid to say so, and I hope his soul finds the peace he was unable to find in his life among the living where he was so worried, anxious and agitated.

I used to say to him: "Calm down! Sit still! Ou kon pwa ka bouyi!"[17]

It was no use.

I don't recall exactly how our paths crossed.

As I don't sleep very much any longer, I'm up before the sun, who's still sprawling somewhere behind the sea, leaving a trace of shadow reigning over the gardens and clinging to the branches while I'm already busy in my kitchen.

I grind my coffee and listen to the little grating song of my coffee mill that I haven't changed for the electric version my son gave me. I let it drip, I pour a few drops onto the ground in memory of my Siméon, with whom I continue to share everything, and I drink it, sitting at my kitchen table, its bitter scent penetrating my nostrils. Then I go out for a walk amid the smell of morning rain in the country. I look in the direction of the sea to find out what color the day will be and then delve into the woods to look for plants to relieve the pain in my old bones. Night has entered my left eye but I can recognize them by their scents, peppery like the star anise, metallic, brackish or bittersweet.

I think that must have been how I came across him one morning. Instead of staying in bed in the warmth of a woman's body he would be up with the sun roving through the woods. He greeted me very politely, for whatever they say about him he was a gentleman and had education. Then he asked me:

"What do they call this plant over here?"

---

[17] *You're like peas on the boil!*

"Let me smell it," I answered. "That's cattail grass."

"I know it by the name of 'diviri.' It works like a charm for diarrhea."

I was amazed.

"How do you know that?"

He laughed with all his fine thirty white teeth.

"Oh, I could tell you a tale or two! I was a doctor. Sometimes my patients were so poor they couldn't afford an aspirin. And then we were far, so far away from the rest of the world. You had to make do. I did miracles with my magnifying glass, my little pestle and mortar. And that's how I got the name 'Curandero.' Today I can say that those years were the best of my life. Out in the woods, with nothing to my name . . ."

Yes, that's how we became friends.

From that time on, once the sun was abed, he would turn up, followed by his shadow, like a dog that never leaves its master, and say:

"How are you feeling in yourself, Mama Sonson?"

"Squeezed to the last drop, as slow as a cart pulled by two oxen tired of climbing the hill of life."

"Come now!" he would protest. "Your eyes are sparkling with youth."

The people who say he was a chatterbox are right. He was always telling you something. But I didn't pay any attention. Except once. I'd heard what he'd just done to Mira and I looked at him and looked at him, and couldn't believe that that face, those two eyes belonged to a scoundrel like so many of the rest of them, like all the rest of them.

"Marry her, marry her," I couldn't help saying. "She didn't deserve this."

He looked up and I saw all the suffering in the world in his eyes.

"I can't, I can't. She mustn't keep the child even. I told her from the very start. But women never listen. I haven't come here to plant children and watch them walk on this earth. I've come to put an end, yes, an end to a race that's cursed. And he's there watching me. You see, Mama Sonson, I told her all that. She's the one to blame. Not me."

I tried to understand what all these words meant and went on:

"Do you mean to say you've got a wife back in your country? Your country's a long way away, Monsieur Francis. You won't find anyone going to look for the other marriage license!"

He shook his head.

"How could I ever be married knowing what I know? I've always avoided women, living as I do on borrowed time."

I burst out laughing.

"Living on borrowed time? I'd change places with you any day!"

He looked out through the window at the blackening square of night and murmured:

"Don't say that, Mama Sonson, don't say that!"

The sound of his voice made my blood run cold.

He didn't deserve such a death. Dying like a dog right in the middle of the path!

People say it was the burden of his sins, known and unknown, that killed him. I don't believe a word.

If only death would come for me too and cover my two eyes, red from sitting up with suffering and mourning, with a thick blanket of black velvet. My body is tired of tossing and turning like a pirogue on the high seas. My bones are cracking.

The night will be long. I've already dozed off in the middle of a Hail Mary, and Mama Rosa woke me up with a little dig in the ribs. She looks relieved, Rosa. Vilma will go back home and nobody will be surprised if Sylvestre, with all his money, manages to marry her off, despite her papaless child. Times have changed!

Poor Francis Sancher, there are not many who will shed a tear for him! Not many who will help him find the door to Eternal Life.

Joby

It's the second time I've seen a dead body, but it's the first time I've been to a wake. I thought wakes didn't exist anymore. I thought they were things old people rambled on about like "When Sorin was governor" or "When I was a child," things that only lived as misty memories in their heads.

When Maman Dinah's mother died, my grandmother on my mother's side, my parents took me with them to Saint-Martin. There was no wake. We arrived by plane mid-morning and a car drove us to the house of the deceased.

There were flowers everywhere. The coffin had been set in the middle of the living room in a sort of metal box and my grandmother was lying at the bottom, all sickly and shriveled up, her eyes half-open and her skin whitened by her long illness. Maman Dinah started to cry and Papa said to her:

"What's the point of crying? That won't bring her back to life."

Everyone had been waiting for us. The undertaker's assistants took the coffin out of the metal box. You could see her old, withered face. Somebody said:

"Oh, we must close her eyes!"

Maman Dinah cried even louder, then she kissed her. Then it was Papa's turn. I rushed out and went and hid in the kitchen under the sink. From there I thought I heard Papa mutter angrily: "Where's that boy got to?"

I closed my eyes. I stayed a long, long time under the sink on my knees among the buckets and wet floorcloths. I was scared. I was hot. Finally it was Marty the servant girl who found me. Very softly, she said:

"You can come out now. They're sealing the coffin. There's no need to kiss her."

I went back to the living room where nobody took any notice of me because they were all crying. The undertakers were using their blowtorches amid the smell of fire and molten metal. At one point, Papa saw me and asked:

"Where were you? Coward!"

For once, Maman Dinah took my defense.

"Leave him alone!" she said.

At the cemetery there were seashells and conch shells painted white, arranged around graves dug into the earth. There were also some impressive tombs, as big as houses. Grandmother's was one of those. There were photos sealed into the marble with names underneath that I couldn't read. I wasn't scared any longer. When we got back to Rivière au Sel, Papa started to call me "chicken" and tell everybody that I had refused to kiss my grandmother. He started saying I was afraid of everything, that Minerve was to blame, the servant girl who nursed me into this world, because she was filling my head with stories about witches, people in league with the devil and people who turn into dogs. It's not true. It's been ages since Minerve stopped telling me stories of that sort. She's become a Seventh-Day Adventist and is very religious. She reads the Bible in her kitchen:

"Now, he told them, remove the foreign gods among you and turn your heart to the Eternal, the God of Israel."

That's why Papa brought me here. So that I would see a corpse and behave like a man.

People say that Francis Sancher didn't have a proper suit and that they had to run up this skimpy black one double quick and buy this tie that is strangling his neck.

It's awful! Since we all have to end up dying, I wonder what's the point of being born. Of being a pretty baby like Quentin, Mira's son.

When Mira gave birth, it was dark. There was no wind that evening. A great silence had fallen from the mountains at dusk. All you could hear was the screech of a few crickets that the servant girls had shut in by mistake and the barking of the dogs in the garden that the watchman had unleashed. I couldn't get to sleep and was thinking of Mira, alone in her room, never seeing anybody, except for Maman Dinah who walks her, leaning on her arm, to the old ornamental pond near the ylang-ylang, when I heard shouts. It was Maman Dinah on the telephone:

"Quick, doctor! She's just lost her waters!"

Lost her waters? What did that mean? I had the impression the Gully had overflowed its banks and was going to rush through the middle of the house, its cold, frothy water carrying drowned toads, goats and dogs. Then Maman Dinah called the servant girls who sleep up in the attic during the week:

"Minerve! Sandra! Cornélia!"

They galloped down the stairs.

I was scared. I went out onto the veranda. In the dark I saw the red glow of Aristide's cigarette as he leaned against a pillar.

"Did you hear?" I said. "She's going to give birth."

"I can hear as well as you can," he shouted. "Clear off!"

So I went into the garden and sat on the steps of the old ornamental pond.

It seems that when Papa was little the pond was full of clear water that came down from the mountains and wound through our garden. The servant girls used to fill their jars from it, because they say you didn't need a Frigidaire in those days. Then a planter diverted the water for his banana grove and the pond has been dry ever since. Just a little moss and lichen at the bottom.

Quentin, Mira's son, was born exactly at midnight. That means he'll be dealing with the spirits.

I wonder if other boys hate their father like I do. I wish he would die. I wish it was him stretched out in front of me instead of Francis Sancher, who also did a lot of harm around him.

In fact, although every day I heard so on and so forth about Francis Sancher, I only saw him once in flesh and blood. It was well before Mira went to live with him and before Quentin was born. As soon as we'd heard he was a Cuban, Papa declared there were too many foreigners in Guadeloupe and that he should be deported with all those Dominicans and Haitians. Lucien Evariste, our French teacher, however, promised us he would invite him to speak on Radyo Kon Lambi because he must have fought in the

Sierra Maestra with Fidel. Lucien Evariste said that we too needed a revolution and a Fidel, but that alas it would never come about. Consumer society has rotted the hearts of the Guadeloupeans, the way sugar has rotted the teeth of the Polynesians.

The one and only time then that I met Francis Sancher was the day I had been punished because my algebra homework had been so terrible. I had stayed behind to redo it in the prep room, which stinks of urine and shit because it's next to the WC's that are always blocked up. So I missed the half past five bus. Instead of waiting for the six o'clock bus, all alone in front of the school that is so close to the cemetery you can see the black and white squares on the tombs, I took a short cut by Grande-Savane. From the top of the hill you get a view of the bay. Over the top of the sea grapes I could see some French French windsurfing and the sea was spotted with red, green and purple. They looked like hot air balloons. Aristide used to take us to the sea and teach us how to float on our backs. He's forgotten about us now. He's even forgotten about his greenhouses. Even though he's got some new orchids, all striped, that they call scorpions. It seems they eat insects. I stepped into the woods. I like the green shadow between the trunks which is the color of moonlight. Here I'm not afraid because I know each tree by its name. I call them and they kneel down for me to climb on their backs and whip them with a branch. We travel through space. Suddenly I saw this man, this stranger, sitting on the root of a tree doing nothing. I guessed at once who it was and said politely:

"Good evening, sir!"

He got up and began to walk beside me, asking me questions, while his giant, ogre's feet crushed ferns and flowers.

"What's your name? How old are you? Are you getting along all right at school?"

It irritated me the way he talked to me like a baby.

"No, I'm not," I said dryly. "My father says I shall end up carting manure like the Haitians."

He shrugged his shoulders.

"Your father shouldn't say such things. The Haitians are a great people. I've met them in America, Angola and a lot in Zaire!"

Immediately, he caught my interest, because I too want to see the world when I grow up.

"Have you visited all those countries?" I asked.

He laughed, but his laugh sounded as sad as a rusty bell in a deserted house.

"Yes, I've been around quite a bit. I've drifted here and there. I've seen the mess ideas of good and evil, justice and injustice, oppression and exploitation can do."

I didn't like what he said. I didn't say anything, but even so he sensed I didn't agree. He put his arm around my shoulder and said:

"Are you interested in politics?"

His arm weighed as heavy as a dead branch.

"Well, a little," I answered.

He burst out laughing.

"Really? Let's sit down a while and I'll tell you about politics." I hesitated, but he dragged me towards a tree stump.

"Have you ever heard of Carlotta?"

"Carlotta?"

"No, of course not, it was before you were born. It was Operation Carlotta that won me over. I was young, I thought it a way of making amends. Father Luandino Vieira, who had held me over the baptismal font, suggested I do it. He told me: 'Atone for your sins, turn over a new leaf. Go forth and clothe those who are naked. Heal those who are suffering.' We arrived by way of Coral Island and if only you could have seen the joy and jubilation! All that cannon fodder cleaning their Soviet guns!"

On hearing all that bla-bla-bla I said:

"Excuse me, sir, but I have to go home now."

But he held me back. His hands were like claws!

"We quickly became disillusioned. I was one of the first. The wounded in the trucks were calling for their mothers and everyone was in a state of bewilderment. So one night I went straight ahead and left and that's how I became 'Curandero.' What do you say here? Doktè fèye?"[18]

I remained silent. I just wanted to leave.

"You too, I bet," he went on, "you'd like to defend the oppressed. But whatever you do they'll hate you. They'll sniff out where you came from and hate you for it. And then there's nothing more savage, you know, nothing more basically despicable than a person who's been downtrodden and then freed from his chains . . ."

I didn't want to hear another word. I wriggled free and began to run. He started to run behind me, but I was faster. I didn't stumble over the buttress roots and I knew how to hold on to the shingle vines.

I could hear him shout:

"Wait for me! Why don't you wait for me?"

But I flew like a bird.

At one point I missed my footing and rolled on the moss. I leaned against a tree trunk to catch my breath and then I saw Xantippe standing a few steps away watching me. My blood froze in my veins as it does every time I see this soucouyant.[19] I don't

---

[18] Leaf doctor.

[19] A spirit that attacks humans and drinks their blood.

know how I got up again. I fled away under the canopy of mountain olives that whispered: "Faster! Faster!"

In the clearing I found myself out of breath face to face with Mademoiselle Léocadie Timothée, who was toddling along taking the evening air and, in the same quavering voice as Monsieur Seguin's goat, said:

"Don't run like that! You'll catch a hot and cold from opening the fridge door to get a glass of iced water when you get home."

I continued to run as fast as my legs would carry me and got back home. I went and sat on the steps of the old ornamental pond and cried hot tears. Why? Because Francis Sancher had told me a lot of nonsense?

I'll tell Lucien Evariste that just because Francis Sancher is a Cuban doesn't mean he fought in the Sierra Maestra.

Yes, Francis Sancher was just as bad as Papa and I can't understand why Mira came to the wake. People will say she has no respect for herself.

Poor Quentin! He'll have no souvenir of his father. Not even a photo. We've got plenty of family pictures. Right back to great-grandfather Gabriel. He was a white planter from Martinique who married a Negro girl. His family disowned him because of that and he came to live in Guadeloupe. That's my favorite photo. He's wearing spectacles and a musketeer's mustache. She's got a pleated madras kerchief and a thick choker. When I grow up I'd like to do a terrible thing like that which would make Papa furious.

But what?

Dinah

"Oh, forget about love, forget about love,

On this earth,

When you've lost your love,

You've got nothing but tears!

Oh, forget about love, forget about love,

On this earth,

When you've lost your love,

You've got nothing but tears!

I took my heart

And gave it to a wretch

To a young man without feeling,

To a young man without love."

My mother would sing this song as she combed her jet-black hair, curiously flecked with auburn. She drew a part from the top of her forehead, then with dollops of Roja brilliantine and water, so that it wouldn't twist around the comb like the vines of the passion fruit, she would bring it sensibly over to cover her ears. As a finishing touch, she would dust off her shoulders with a small, ivory-handled brush, dab Soir de Paris on her neck and go off to sit behind the till in my stepfather's shop. She used to close the cash register at half past twelve exactly and return at two. She was born in Philipsburg of Dutch blood[20] and hated the inhabitants of Marigot, whom she called "crude and coarse, like their masters, the French." When she was young her father had sent her to study in Amsterdam and she was always telling me about the Rijksmuseum and its wonderful Rembrandts, the lazy, shimmering water of the canals and the reflection of the stern façades of the stone houses between the barges. Instead of studying pharmacy, however, she had a child, none other than me, by an Indonesian student, whom she described as the son of a sultan, but who in real life was no doubt poor and just as lonely and as lost as she was, shivering under those sunless skies. Her father had her brought back to the island and was only too happy to marry her off to my stepfather, a prosperous businessman, but a widower, burdened with five children, who made her suffer enormously. So when Loulou Lameaulnes came visiting with his high forehead and thinning hair, wearing a starched, white drill suit, she summed up the situation immediately and said to me:

"He's got three good-for-nothing boys and an illegitimate girl. All he's looking for is a servant to take care of them. A servant, that's what you'll be!"

I didn't listen to her, because you never listen to your mother,

---

[20] *The island of Saint-Martin is divided into the French side and the Dutch side.*

and at that time, Loulou had dreamy brown eyes. My stepfather liked Loulou because he spoke with authority:

"The Guadeloupe of yesteryear died a natural death. Those who put blinkers over their eyes, those who still believe in sugarcane are crazy. My great-grandfather Gabriel deserves a statue. He was the first to see the light and set up these nurseries. They laughed at him. 'You can't eat flowers, Monsieur Lameaulnes,' they said. And after that the nurseries were always inherited by those who were thought to be no good, like my poor father, like myself, like Aristide after me. Let them say what they like! Soon there will be the Single European Market and I shall sell my flowers as far away as England. Yes, my flowers will decorate the table of the Queen of England. Her Majesty the Queen. I've already got my slogan: 'The Lameaulnes Nurseries: an earthly paradise for flowers.' "

After he left, my stepfather nodded his head.

"There's a man who knows what he wants."

When I arrived at Rivière au Sel I was in a state of joy. I didn't hear the women untangling their hair on their porch whisper:

"There goes the girl from Saint-Martin, there goes the girl from Saint-Martin."

I didn't see the children shy away when I fondled them. I wanted to work at the nurseries. All those flowers, all those plants whose scent and color made me feel dizzy! But Loulou was against it.

"The Lameaulnes ladies have always had enough to do at home."

So I stayed at home with my servants, my children, and gradually this house made of wood at the edge of the dense forest, deprived of light and sun, a paradise dripping with lover's chains and anthuriums, this house became my prison, my tomb. My youth flew away. At times, it seemed I was already dead and my blood had already frozen in my veins.

It's been years since Loulou slept in my bed. Once darkness has fallen I lock my door and curl up like a fetus between my sheets.

It's on nights when the wind gets up, when it throws branches and unripe fruit to the ground, when it flattens the cabins and sends sheets of tin roofing flying, that I tremble the most. My prayers to God remain unanswered. I call for help to all those who loved me but are now gone. I imagine my father, brown-skinned and distinguished like pandit Nehru; my mother, the gentle Lina, her eyes always brimming with tears. They respond to my call. They sit at my bedside and comfort me, telling me the stories I heard when I was young:

"At that time—I'm talking of a long, long time ago, a 'once upon a time' time—it was the moon that was in charge. Every morning she leaned out of the sky and looked at the earth, saying: 'If you ask me, we need a river here. A row of royal palms there. A bush of red ixoras over there.' And her will was done."

I listen to them, I listen to them and finally sleep carries me off around five in the morning, when the sun's rays are already coloring the louvered shutters and the servant girls are moving about in the attic.

Nobody knows that I am to blame for the tragedy that has just drawn to a close. But I am, and nobody else.

The misfortunes of the children are always caused by the secret sins of the parents.

It was the servant girls I first heard talking about Francis Sancher. Cornélia was telling Gitane how he had been looking everywhere for a carpenter and had come to ask Marval, her husband, to help him. She said that Marval wouldn't do anything of the sort, not for all the gold in Guyana. That same day at lunch

Loulou shouted he ought to be deported with the Dominicans and Haitians. To this Aristide retorted that he was only too happy to have the Dominicans and Haitians do the work at the nurseries that no Guadeloupean deigned to do. As usual they started to argue and a torrent of abuse flowed out of Loulou's mouth.

After lunch, when Dodose Pélagie brought me a recipe for sweet potato pie, she complained that her unfortunate son, Sonny, spent all his time at Francis Sancher's.

In the end, curiosity got the better of me and I went to see for myself what the man who was putting Rivière au Sel into such a commotion looked like.

A man was chatting with Moïse the postman. Very tall. Very strong. Bent over, he was a head taller than Moïse and broader by both shoulders. Despite its being a cool evening, he was bare-chested and you could see the hard outline of his pectorals above a forest of jet-black hair that contrasted with the gray mane on his head. His arms were bicolored. Almost black up to the elbow, then golden above. I couldn't help thinking:

"Oh, Lord! Imagine a hunk of a man like that in your bed night after night!"

At that very moment he turned towards me and his eyes plunged into mine as if he were reading my thoughts. I wanted to hurry on by, but I was nailed to the spot in front of the hedge of rayo. He greeted me.

His face was of a rich, roasted corn color. His eyes held the promise of long journeys. His mouth, that of never-ending kisses. After so many years, I had ended up forgetting that I was a woman and I was frightened of the desires that were flaring up inside of me.

I ran home as fast as I could. But that same evening, with doors and windows shut tight, he came and joined me. And the night after and the night after that . . .

Thanks to Francis Sancher, I no longer saw nor heard Loulou. He could pass me by, do what he liked with my servants up in the attic above my head, give orders, shout insults, I no longer cared about all that. Sometimes, I had sudden misgivings and went down on my knees to ask the Good Lord to forgive me. However, as soon as dusk descended I forgot my remorse and was carried away by my dreams.

One night, after we had made love, I remained clinging to his side like seaweed and we talked in the dark. I told him about Loulou.

"Does it make sense to you? What have I done to him? Why did he bring me all the way from Philipsburg to treat me the way he does? Haven't I got light skin? Isn't my hair black and curly? Haven't I given him three lovely boys? I haven't committed any crime. Shouldn't he treat me rather like the Holy Sacrament?"

He covered my face with kisses.

"My little angel, that's how we are, we men! Neither the skin nor the hair have anything to do with it. The white women in French France suffer the same. It's the fate of all women. We're born torturers. But you're still young and beautiful. Why do you put up with it? Why don't you leave?"

Leave? Where would I go?

How long did this paltry happiness last?

The night Mira ran away I waited for him in vain. The following night I did the same. Then Moïse came to tell us that she'd gone to live with him. With Francis Sancher! Mira's like my daughter. When I arrived at Loulou's I loved her at first sight, a wild little thing with a bleeding heart. I too grew to understand her and I prayed, I prayed to the Good Lord He would pardon her sin, however horrible it was, and send her a savior to deliver her from her jail.

Why did she have to take Francis Sancher from me? Precisely the man who was an oasis in my desert?

Hatred burnt up my heart, like the savanna in the dry season. I called down misfortune on her, and Satan, who is always on the lookout, heard me, for she came back with her belly, her shame and her pain.

I am the cause of all this distress. I am and nobody else. Since she didn't suspect anything she confided in me. But instead of arousing my jealousy the story she told me brought water to my eyes:

"I was never happy with him. Even when his body was on top of mine, I knew his mind was wandering in regions I could never reach.

"Sometimes I would lose my temper with him.

" 'Don't I exist in your two eyes?' I said to him. 'Speak to me!'

"He shrugged his shoulders.

" 'About what? I no longer have bow, spear or arrow. I've lost all my combats. Soon I shall lose the last, the combat of life.'

"He crossed over to the window and murmured:

" 'Can't you see him lying in wait for me?'

"I went up to him and replied:

" 'I can't see anything but a trail of fireflies zigzagging in the dark.'

"Or: 'All I can see is Xantippe looking for his rabbit feed.'

" 'You have two eyes to see nothing with.'

"When I told him I was missing my blood, he became gentle, almost tender. I told myself it was the miracle of the baby. It's been known to happen before.

"Every morning he made me drink a tea that he had concocted himself with leaves he went and picked amid the dew, and roots he left to macerate in alcohol. He maintained it would give me strength. But in fact I felt weaker and weaker. I vomited blood and phlegm. Sometimes I fell into a state. One evening he gave me a very bitter herb tea, and sleep carried me off at once. My spirit left my body, peacefully, peacefully. It seemed I had come back to live in the shady womb of my mother, Rosalie Sorane, with her teeth of pearl. I was floating, swimming with happiness in her uterine sea and I could hear far away the sad, muffled sounds of a world I had made up my mind never to enter. Suddenly, I was stabbed with a terrible pain. I woke up and saw him leaning over me. He was brutally opening my legs with one hand, and with the other he was trying to stick a long, sparkling needle into me. When he realized I had woken up he began to whine and stammer: 'That child must never open its eyes to the light of day. Never. An ill omen is upon him as it is upon me. He'll live a life of calamities and he'll end up dying like a dog as I shall soon do. I have come here to end it all. To come full circle. To put the finishing touches, you understand. Return to square one and stop everything. When the coffee tree is riddled with greenfly and only bears black, stony fruit it has to be burnt.' "

A sad story that I compared to my own life. I'd believed he was different but this man too was nothing but a murderer. A torturer, he had said it himself. An insidious feeling, something I'd never felt before, a sense of revolt, was growing inside of me. I kept turning over and over again a question he had asked me. Why do we put up with it? Yes, why? I asked myself, day and night.

One evening Aristide gave a loud kick at the bedroom door and shouted:

"Do you know who he's got in his bed that's still warm from the last person? Oh, he hasn't wasted much time! Vilma, Vilma Ramsaran!"

It was there and then that I made up my mind.

Around me the women are praying:

"I counted the dead happy because they were dead, happier

than the living who are still in life. More fortunate than either I reckoned the man yet unborn, who had not witnessed the wicked deeds done here under the sun."

I have made a decision. I'm going to leave Loulou and Rivière au Sel. I'll take my boys with me. I'm going to look for the sun and the air and the light for what's left of the years to live.

Where will I find them? I don't know yet. What I do know is that I'm going to look for them.

Sonny

Staring at the coffin, Sonny chanted the grief that was overflowing his heart. His mother, seated on his right, pressed his hand tightly and he tried to hold back the sounds of his pain. The others round about once again asked themselves why Dodose had insisted on bringing this unfortunate boy who upset the children and scared pregnant women. They maintained it was his fault that Luciana, Lucien the carpenter's young bride, had carried a dead child around for months before giving birth one morning much to her husband's great distress. She had come face to face with Sonny and had been taken with a seizure. After that, her baby's blood had curdled in her womb!

Dodose, who had always refused to look the truth in the face—despite what the doctors in La Pointe had told her plus a trip to Paris to see a specialist at the Salpêtrière hospital—had taken Sonny to school when he was old enough. Mademoiselle Léocadie Timothée, who was still working at the time, had come to see her one evening to beg her to keep Sonny at home. He was bothering the other children.

While Dodose showered her with a torrent of abuse and called down the wrath of the Good Lord on this heartless woman who had never known the warmth of a man's embrace and didn't know what it was to be a mother, Sonny had cried his heart out. In what way did he bother the other children, he who sat at the back of the class, sang only to himself and drew pictures on his paper? To avoid being laughed at during recreation, he didn't venture out into the school yard, but remained sitting at the same place, trying to make himself as small as possible.

So he made a resolution. Without telling anyone, he stuffed his satchel each morning with slates, crayons, exercise books and ballpoints and went off. Nevertheless he realized he had to remain at a fair distance from the school, near enough to see the little girls whose hair combed into "vanilla pods" and carefully brilliantined braids glistened in the sun, far enough not to draw the attention of the teachers or, worse still, of the boys who hurled stones and the word "estèbekouè."[21]

He had soon discovered an excellent observation point: the veranda of the Alexis house. From there you could hear every shriek a child made until the bell rang and silence suddenly fell. Perched on the balustrade, you looked down on the row of classrooms.

---

[21] Lunatic.

Sonny had a stock of songs in his head and he himself didn't know where they came from. He started in the early morning on opening his eyes, invariably full of sleep, and was hardly affected by his father's yelling.

"Dodose, get your son to shut up!"

He continued through the hours of daylight. There were songs for every moment of the day; songs for when the sun was still stretching and yawning above the sea, for when it dazzled everything triumphantly high in the sky, when it sprawled lazily, mouth open, on the clouds, and when finally it descended to gorge itself on blood behind the mountains. The songs, however, stopped when night came, when Sonny was consumed by a raging fear.

When night came, Dodose was tired, very tired of repeating every day to comfort him:

"There, there, it's nothing! That's an ATR 42 flying to Martinique. That sound is the branch of the mango tree scraping against the top of the water tank."

But her words had no effect! Sonny remained sweating and shaking, his eye following an invisible cavalcade into space.

The realm of daylight had nothing in common with that of the dark. It was an enchantment of light reflected in the puddles of the potholes, the dewdrops clinging to the grass and the secrets of the tall trees in the cool of the woods.

Sonny knew every forest path. When school was over he would walk up to the top of the hill at Dillon, puffing and sweating after two long hours. Up there, he felt himself a king, towering above the stunted vegetation poorly nourished by the laterite soil. He would pick armfuls of hog plums, thorn flowers and guavas that he couldn't help taking home to Dodose, knowing full well that she would throw them all away sighing:

"Where have you been raking up all that muck?"

He loved nothing better than the days when the wind would

get up without warning and the rain would sweep through like a warm blessing from the sky.

The untamed realm of the night, however, was dark and forbidding. Spirits hid there, betrayed only by the reflection of their big protruding eyes.

Sonny was certain his parents were at odds because of him. Emmanuel only spoke to Dodose to give orders or to level blame at her. To complain for example of a crease in his shirt. To demand a brush to polish his shoes over again. To question the freshness of the red snapper. Although Dodose had her chats with Madame Mondésir or Madame Ramsaran on the veranda, Emmanuel had nobody. Except for Agénor Siméus. Every Saturday, the double gates were left open and, at 4 p.m. precisely, Agénor Siméus drove up the drive bordered with dwarf coconut trees and parked his Peugeot 506 at the bottom of the steps. He would haul himself out, pat Sonny's cheek in passing, even though Sonny was now a head taller than he was, throw him a hearty "How's it going, young man?" and go and sit down with Emmanuel in the living room. Emmanuel would fetch two glasses and a bottle of Glenfiddich and then switch on the stereo that nobody was allowed to touch, which he had bought in Manaus at a meeting of rain forest experts. Then he inserted a compact disc with the precautions of a midwife handling a newborn baby. Madame Butterfly wailed a few moments, then Agénor Siméus asked:

"Have you read the latest issue of the *Magazine Caraibe?*"

"You know full well I don't read that bullshit!" he thundered.

So Agénor would put on his glasses, draw out of his pocket a few crumpled sheets of paper and start to read some long-winded Open Letter addressed by an angry citizen to some politician or other. Emmanuel listened in deep silence and then concluded:

"There's only ever been one honest politician in this country, and that's Rosan Girard!"

Agénor jumped up.

"But you're forgetting Légitimus!"

"Him honest?"

And the verbal sparring would begin; the Socialists, the Communists, the Patriots and the Assimilationists would each get a dressing-down.

At half past six, the shadows would start to fill the living room and Emmanuel would get his breath back to shout:

"Dodose, we can't see a thing!"

While Dodose fussed about, Agénor Siméus would get up on his two feet and take leave of everyone.

This was the sign for the servant girl to come out of the kitchen and announce: "Manjé la pawé!" (Food's on the table!)

One morning, the sun rose as brilliant and sparkling as it always did. The mountains were green. The sky, a faded blue. Sonny grabbed a bottle of kerosene, stuffed his satchel with rags and set off for the Alexis house. The more Rivière au Sel set about fearing and avoiding it, the more the Alexis house became his domain, his property. The spirits who lived there were all on his side and had never bothered him, even during the long siestas he took during the afternoon, curled up on the cool tiles of the veranda. He set off, hopping as usual across a copse carpeted crimson with herbaceous phanerogams.

When he came out onto the road, he couldn't believe his eyes. The house, his house, was open.

A stranger was standing on the veranda beside Moïse, the postman, who, on seeing Sonny, savagely shouted:

"Clear off!"

Then went on to explain to his companion:

"That's Dodose Pélagie's son; she's the biggest pain in the neck in Rivière au Sel. You'll soon make her acquaintance. She can hear a safety pin drop in a bedroom!"

The stranger smiled.

"What do they call you?"

And as Sonny stood there, mute, dribbling, fidgeting and grotesque, Moïse said:

"Can't you see he's crazy?"

Who knows why and how the little seed of friendship takes root and starts to bud? Sonny ought to have hated Francis Sancher for having burst into his kingdom and plundered it. Instead of which he found a friend. Somebody who tried to decipher his mumblings. Who wiped his brow and his lips compassionately with a handkerchief. Who painted life with the colors of travel and adventure.

Under the contemptuous gaze of Moïse, set on demonstrating that in his eyes Sonny was nothing but a repulsive worm, Francis Sancher would clap time in rhythm with the boy's voice and declare:

"You're a marvelous musician!"

Francis Sancher also liked his drawings.

"What an imagination you have! Where did you get the idea for this from?" he asked.

One day he exclaimed:

"Good Lord! Have you ever been to Italy? It looks like the Villa Melzi on the edge of Lake Como!"

Sonny was no longer ever alone! Clinging to his friend's big warm hand, he would stride through the woods, looking up at the trees plumed with silvery leaves.

"Is it true what they say?" Francis Sancher questioned him as if he expected an answer for real. "Is it true that the gum tree is so called because it secretes a gum ideal for making pirogues for the high seas? Is it true that a tiny decoction of that tree's bark makes our sword rise invincible?"

As soon as the shadows started to lengthen they would return to Rivière au Sel, for Francis Sancher shared his terror of the night. He would quicken his step.

"Hurry! Hurry! Soon they will be breaking their chains!"

They both had the same terror of Xantippe. Whenever he saw him prowling across the savanna or standing rigid under some bay tree Francis Sancher would stammer:

"Did you see him? Did you see him?"

Sometimes they found the poor devil along the rayo hedge, watching them hazily. Francis Sancher would then barricade himself inside.

"He's followed me everywhere. When I forded the rivers he was there. When I was up to my waist in the swamps, he stuck to me like a leech. One night I pleaded with him: 'Don't you know the meaning of forgiveness? The fault is a very ancient one. I'm not the one to be blamed directly. Why do the children's teeth always have to be on edge?' "

Moïse interrupted him with a glass of rum.

"Now, now! Stop talking through the top of your head!"

Francis Sancher emptied his glass, wiped his mouth with the back of his hand and pleaded:

"It wasn't me, it wasn't me who shed his blood before hanging him from the manjack tree!"

At times like these, seeing him shake like a child, Sonny, suddenly tall, strong and handsome, felt torrents of love well up from his heart to comfort his friend.

Sonny had got into the habit of picking a few Bourbon oranges or starfruit still fresh with the dew from Dodose's garden to go with their breakfast. One morning, as he arrived with his daily offering, whom did he see seated at the table on the veranda facing Francis Sancher? None other than Mira Lameaulnes.

There she was, proudly glowing with her light skin that made others ashamed of the color of theirs. Glowing with her dazzling shock of hair. Glowing with her scent of forbidden fruit.

If ever anyone had laughed at, martyred and hounded Sonny with her spitefulness, it was Mira. When she stopped in front of the church with her parents for the weekly gossip, her prying, alley-cat eyes would burn him with contempt. Once when she had met him up on the hill at Dillon, she had picked up a stick to threaten him with, although he was only looking at her.

Who had transplanted this poisonous manchineel onto his shores?

"Get out of here!" she had already started to bark.

Sonny took to his heels while Francis Sancher got up and shouted:

"Wait! Wait, let me explain!"

Explain what? What was there to explain?

After this betrayal, Sonny never saw Francis Sancher again. He never again took the road to the Alexis house. In fact, he hardly ever left his room and his bed, staring at the pattern of the beams above his head and singing himself songs of consolation.

When Dodose, worried out of her mind, had taken him to see a specialist in La Pointe, the doctor, a French Frenchman with eyes the color of rainwater, had examined him for one whole hour before pronouncing his case hopeless.

His friend was dead!

Amid the glow of candles around him the women's faces grimaced, like those masks that used to scare him when Dodose took him to the carnival in La Pointe, thinking it would amuse him.

A piercing song burst forth from his lips, and Dodose, having pressed his hand in vain, resigned herself to taking him out onto the veranda.

Deafened by the noise of the rain, the men had drawn their chairs up close and were laughing, heads together. Leaning up against a column, oblivious to all the noise, Loulou Lameaulnes was staring into space.

Loulou

The Queen of England, Elizabeth II, is sitting with her crown of diamonds planted squarely on her head at the end of a long, rectangular table decorated with flowers from Guadeloupe. There are nursery flowers, of course, arum lilies, orchids, mainly spathoglottis plicata from Malaysia, as well as striped scorpion flowers on long, curved spikes, lilies of the Virgin with heavy, bluish petals, torch lilies that seem to have been set artificially at the end of their straight, leafless stems, Barbados lilies and roses; but also hardy, wild flowers, surprising the eye with their unexpected bloom:

the seaside potato, the leaf of life that flowers in the undergrowth behind the beach, the goosefoot creeper, the yellow heliconia, the red heliconia and many, many others.

The Queen of England smiles at me, she has a tooth filled with gold from Guyana in her lower jaw, and says to me:

"Are you the one growing all these flowers?"

I nod my head and she asks:

"What is the name of your nurseries?"

"Since 1905 they have carried the family name," I answer. "The Lameaulnes Nurseries."

So the Queen of England says:

"Bravo! Henceforth, you shall be our purveyor. By appointment to Her Majesty Queen Elizabeth II . . ."

For over thirty years, as soon as he closed his eyes, Loulou had been having the same dream. That's how he realized he had fallen asleep amid the murmurs of the rain and the night, amid the chattering interspersed with laughter from the men and the hum of prayers from the women.

He had no idea where this interest in the Royal Family came from nor why this dream was set on haunting him. The first time it had happened, he had woken up all bewildered beside Melissa, his mistress at the time, who was sleeping like a log, a trickle of shiny saliva dribbling from the corner of her mouth. His mother was still alive, locked in her unfair preference for his younger brother Paolo. When the dream came back a second time, he had told himself that perhaps it was a sign of things to come that would bring a smile to those lips forever pinched as far as he was concerned. His mother would understand his love for her. She would appreciate his efforts. But the years had gone by and the dream had never materialized.

Loulou felt like going home to a warm bed. How could he ever pretend he missed Francis Sancher and not wish him to burn in the sea of hell after a terrible crossing? He the atheist, who no longer believed in all this religious nonsense, saw himself again as the credulous child whose mother's maledictions made him tremble.

"You'll end up in jail! If the Good Lord doesn't punish you in this world, it'll be in the next! He'll get you in the end!"

Why hadn't she loved him? Once again, Loulou asked himself the question. Once again, he couldn't find an answer. Taking advantage of a lull in the running fire of jokes, he got up with his glass full, before the volley started again. Jerbaud, the stonemason, had already cleared his throat and was starting a "Méssié kouté, kouté . . ." (Listen, Gentlemen, listen . . .)

Oh, no, it wasn't jokes that were buzzing through his head. It was bitter, vengeful thoughts, murderous thoughts regarding this malevolent corpse who, when alive, had poisoned his life.

"No, no, no! That's not the way he should have died. His death had been too clean, too gentle. They should have found him with his brains shot out, splattered among the trumpet vines, soaking the lichen and moss with his blood. Since Aristide didn't have the guts, I'm the one who should have done it. But I didn't do anything either."

He took a gulp of rum and the liquid seared his palate and burned all the way down his esophagus. Nevertheless, he was shaking. From the cold and damp, since the rain had not let up. Not only was it dripping onto this Panama hat which he was perhaps one of the last to wear in Guadeloupe, but a genuine pool was lapping at his feet, ensconced in the patent leather boots he had been ordering from a shop in New Orleans for over thirty years. He had gone to New Orleans on his honeymoon with his first wife, and since poor Aurore had never been in very good health—she was dead at thirty, to prove it—the coffee and doughnuts of the French Quarter had laid her up in her hotel room. So he had gone out walking alone, unimpressed by this town which he thought looked like Cap-Haïtien where he had family. Rounding a street corner he had come across a bootmaker. A pair of magnificent boots in the shop window! One hundred dollars at the time! He had paid for them without haggling. It was his only good memory of a ten-day tête-à-tête with a completely useless wife.

He took another swig of rum, asked himself what he was doing here, listening to these coarse jokes, these tales told over a hundred times before and this droning of hypocritical prayers. Why does death have this power? Why does it silence hatreds, violence and bitterness and force us to bend down on two knees when it turns up? And even more than that, it hastens to transform people's minds. Soon someone will probably start to embroider a legend around Francis Sancher and make him out to be a misunderstood hero.

Oh, yes, Rivière au Sel's memory had had no trouble turning his great-grandfather Gabriel, the one who set up the nurseries, into a man with an open heart, who in his generosity gave work to everyone. Whereas in reality this devil of a man, who had been rejected by his family because he had married a Negro girl, detested the niggers in his employ and made them feel it. Besides, he took after his predecessors. The first of the Lameaulnes, Dieudonné Désiré, the owner of a sugar plantation near Marin in Martinique, used to take aim at his slaves' heads and fire bullets into them, doubling up with laughter at their final grimace. Loulou should have been born in those days when might was right. Not in the days of Social Security and Family Allowances. Two weeks earlier a lackey from the Labor Inspectorate had come up to see him. He had heard that the nurseries were employing illegal Haitian workers and had warned Loulou that he could incur heavy penalties. Fines. Imprisonment. Loulou had almost shoved his French back into his mouth.

Yes, he should have been born in another age. Or else in another country. Guadeloupe was too small for him. It did not allow a man to show what he is capable of. Australia! That's where he should have been born. Vast stretches of virgin land burnt by the sun. Struggling hand to hand with Nature, rebellious as a teenager forced into love.

Such is the popular imagination. It transforms a man, whitens him or blackens him to the point that his own mother, the woman who gave him birth, cannot recognize him.

What had it turned his brother Paolo into? A talented poet, an artist, because he had obtained a mention in a poetry contest for one sonnet. Whereas he, Loulou, passed for the idiot in the family.

When he was sixteen, his father, Ferdinand, had been struck dead by a bee sting on his neck, and his uncles, who had always treated their brother little better than a bitako,[22] nicknaming him Kakabef,[23] because he had stayed behind to work the family property at Rivière au Sel, and seating him at the very bottom of the family table, had decided that, after all, this land was perhaps worth something in the banana boom. They had therefore pestered his widow out of her mind to get rid of it and then entrust them with the money from the sale and with the education of her two boys. Mathilda would have accepted, tired, so tired as she was with two boys on her hands who did not get along at all and fought like wild dogs. But Loulou, with all his sixteen years, had said:

---

[22] *Peasant.*

[23] *Cow pie.*

"I'll look after everything."

And he had kept his word.

He had quit the lycée Carnot, where he was no worse than anyone else in mathematics, and had given up a life of pleasure. He would get up at four in the morning, when the night still had the horizon under lock and key, and toil under the sun till evening, when he would grope his way to bed, too tired to screw any woman or even think about it.

Meanwhile, Paolo flunked his baccalauréat three then four times, stayed in bed until noon, bad-talked about him behind his back and had himself pampered by their mother. Until the day he took out the old Peugeot and went and crashed it into one of the pink cedars on the edge of the road. Ever since that day his mother had been in deep mourning and, meal after meal, had sat on the other side of the table, her eyes locked in reproach, as if he had pushed the car with his own two hands.

Yet the reputation of the Lameaulnes Nurseries grew. Orders for his anthuriums came from Nice, Cherbourg and Paris. His roses perfumed the gardens of the Préfecture and his casuarinas shaded the public parks. But nobody was in the least grateful for that. Nobody appreciates the values of endurance and perseverance.

The rain, driven by the wind, soaked his trousers. He stood up, now obliged to take refuge inside the house, and his gaze met that of Aristide, huddled up like an animal about to break his leash. His hatred for his son boiled in his heart. He remembered with contempt their visit to Francis Sancher when he had been laid out in the dust. It was after that visit he had made up his mind to act alone.

Alone.

He had told himself that threats and violence were of no avail, and he had prepared a little speech in his head. Out early while the field-workers were still dragging their feet wretchedly to their instruments of labor, he had found Francis Sancher disheveled, sleeping off a hangover on the veranda. Mira, like a servant, was washing down the steps.

He had been convincing, begging even.

"Listen to what I have to say. We're both on the same side. The history books call our ancestors the Discoverers. Okay, they soiled their blood with Negro women; in your case, it must have been Indian. And yet we've got nothing in common with these nappy-head niggers, these peasants who have always handled a machete or driven an oxcart for us. Don't treat Mira as if she were the child of one of these good-for-nothings."

Francis Sancher had looked at him straight in the eye for a long time, then said in a decided tone of voice:

"You're mistaken. We're no longer on the same side and what's more I don't belong to any side. And yet, to a certain extent, you're right. To start off with, it's true, we were on the same side. That's why I left for the other side of the world. I can't say the journey ended successfully. I was shipwrecked, washed up on the shore . . ."

Loulou had first listened politely. Yet realizing how far Francis Sancher was straying from the subject, he had brought him back to the beaten track.

"Don't talk rubbish when I've come to speak to you about my daughter."

Francis Sancher had then walked up to him. Fearing he was in for the same fate as Aristide, Loulou wished he had brought along the gun he used for shooting thrushes. But Francis Sancher hadn't laid a finger on him, merely spitting out in his face:

"You call that rubbish? Of course, you wouldn't understand. Now clear off!"

Thereupon Mira had slowed the scrubbing movement of her brush and begged:

"Go away! Please go away!"

Loulou had returned home, wondering who was taking his or her revenge. His mother, locked forever in her blind preference? Paolo, deprived of his youth and making him pay for it? Aurore Dugazon, to whom he had given so little consideration? For the first time, he the tireless fighter, who in thirty-five years had treated himself twice to a ten-day vacation, first when he had taken Aurore Dugazon to New Orleans, only to see her take to her hotel bed because of a coffee and doughnuts, and then when he had taken Dinah to Amsterdam, a damp city, which was a fine choice for her sanctimonious kind since the whores flaunted themselves half-naked in red-lighted loggias—he wanted to put an end to everything. He wanted to lay down his old bones in the marble prison of the Lameaulnes vault under the compassionate casuarinas.

When the affair had taken an appalling turn for the worse and Mira had returned home with her belly, leaving Vilma, Vilma Ramsaran, a mere child whose confirmation had been celebrated a few years earlier, to take her place, Loulou went into a frenzy and concluded that it could only be Paolo. Only he was capable of deploying such malice. He had gone to find Sylvestre Ramsaran, who had sung "Maréchal, nous voilà" with him every July 14 in Governor Sorin's time. He never knew quite how to address him, for although one had as much money as the other, they were not of the same race. Twenty years earlier, a Ramsaran would have kept his eyes lowered in front of a Lameaulnes. Brought together by the same misfortune as fathers, he had asked him worriedly:

"What do you intend to do?"

Sylvestre had gestured his powerlessness.

"Carmélien and Jacques want to finish him off. But their maman is asking what would be the point of having two boys in jail as well. Since Vilma is not yet eighteen, we could press charges, but all we'll get is our name in *France-Antilles.*"

"So you're just going to sit idly by?"

There had been silence. Then Sylvestre had resumed mysteriously:

"Moïse says he's hiding stolen money in a trunk."

Loulou had shrugged his shoulders and gone on his way.

The chain of mountains was adorned with the fleeting green of days without rain. For the water that had fallen from the sky to fill jars, drums and barrels had temporarily slaked Nature's thirst. Two dark red-necked hummingbirds were piercing the hearts of the hibiscus. His majesty the sun was keeping watch over his kingdom.

Deep in his thoughts, Loulou had first passed Xantippe, whom he hadn't even looked at, and then two women, whom the bus had set down at the crossroads and who were climbing the steep hill.

"Say what you like," they couldn't help commenting, "misfortune has its own justice! Not only does it take care of those who don't have a penny to their name or are as black as you and me. It punches left and right. Punching the po chappé,[24] the mulattoes, the Indians and, from what I hear, even the whites over there in French France! There goes a man who used to walk upright, so upright that you'd never think that one day he'd be laid in a hole like the rest of us. Now look at him!"

And it was true, Loulou had aged. All he needed was blood-

---

[24] *People of mixed blood.*

shot eyes and a pipe stuck between blackened tooth stumps to look like an old bag of bones.

Loulou looked around for a chair and with a frown got the unfortunate Sonny to give up his seat. Sonny had calmed down and was sighing in rhythm to the chanting of the women.

"For everything its season, and for every activity under heaven its time: a time to be born and a time to die . . ."

He took a glass from the hands of Mademoiselle Léocadie Timothée who had got up and was shakily serving drinks, while her old head nodded gently from her great age and her mouth murmured in prayer.

Sylvestre Ramsaran

"Carmélien and Jacques wanted to polish him off. Rosa wept, saying there was no point having two boys in jail as well. In the end she was right because today the Good Lord has done justice."

At the thought of this justice sent from heaven without having to go and fetch it, Sylvestre Ramsaran couldn't help smirking triumphantly, although it was hardly fitting at a deathbed. But how could he pretend to be grief-stricken when he wasn't?

This little smirk did not escape the attention of the others and reinforced the opinion in Rivière au Sel that Sylvestre Ramsaran's heart had been completely spoiled by money. He did not take after Rodrigue, his father, who had had such a good reputation that the poor would line up in front of his kitchen twice a day at meal times. Once death has cut a man down, in fact, there's no need for bitterness or desire for revenge. Sylvestre Ramsaran, therefore, had no right to triumph openly over Francis Sancher. Sylvestre knew what people thought about him and was none the worse for it. On the contrary. He was glad for his buffalo hide! It had taken him years of hardship to fashion it.

He had started to piece it together and sew it up as a little boy after that disastrous first visit to the temple. Sylvestre was merely the fourth son of Rodrigue Ramsaran. So he didn't really interest his father. He went on living his life at school as a quiet dunce whom the teachers interrogated once a month for form's sake, never even bothering to send him into detention. On Thursdays he would roam freely with other boys of his age, aiming at birds with his slingshot, trying to catch them with glue or picking bunches of wildflowers for his mother whom he worshiped. One day when he was coming back from the woods with his belly showing and his face sticky from mango juice, his father had cast his eyes on him in surprise.

"Danila, how old is that boy now?"

Danila, whose hands were red from plucking a chicken, had made a quick calculation in her head.

"He'll be ten on September second!"

"Ten!"

The following Sunday—orders were orders—Danila had

dressed him in white, combed a part into his thick black hair and whispered in his ear with undefinable pride:

"Today you're going to the temple with your papa!"

To the temple? The word meant nothing to him. Sylvestre had, indeed, got a glimpse in his parents' room, where he never went, of pictures in loud colors, framed with garlands of multicolored lightbulbs, depicting women with a thousand snaky arms, others holding a sort of guitar in one hand and a flower in the other, and characters with an elephant's trunk wound above their potbellied stomachs. All that had nothing to do with him and was part of the disquieting and mysterious realm of grown-ups.

The temple wasn't anything to look at: a cabin topped by a red flag which the rain had soaked and wrapped like a rag around its mast. Yet the veneration of the faces around him convinced him that something big was going to happen. Soon the smell of incense rose up while the noise of cymbals and drums got gradually louder. It was like being in a dream and Sylvestre couldn't say what fascinated him the most: the chanting of the priests or the smell of the flowers, the candles or the camphor burning on a tray. Knowing nothing about his people's past, his imagination had never escaped beyond the sparkling horizon of the island. But now he felt mysteriously transported to a foreign land—murmuring and sweet-smelling like the sea.

It was then that a group of young boys dressed in white had led in the bleating, reluctant goats. They were made to smell the incense, then with one blow, wham! their heads were sliced off. Their little heads with innocent eyes flew into the air while their blood gushed out over the soil. A scream then went up, but Sylvestre didn't know whether it came from his mouth or not, while a burning stream of urine soaked and soiled his fine, white drill trousers.

From that day on Sylvestre had been the-boy-who-had-shamed-his-papa. Every time the Ramsarans got together they dug up this story. With their mouths full of colombo[25] they would add all sorts of fantastic details and half truths, with the result that Sylvestre no longer knew whether he had vomited, urinated or defecated; if he had screamed or if he had run away terrified to the other end of the savanna. It was to erase those images that Sylvestre had become a fervent Hindu, celebrating samblmani[26] and divapali[27] alike, and shaving the heads of his children on the banks of the river Moustique. Alas, all to no avail. The eighty-year-old Rodrigue would still repeat with his head nodding up and down:

"I fè mwen ront tou bonman! Sé ront i fè mwen ront!" (He made me feel so ashamed! So ashamed!)

When Sylvestre Ramsaran, by the sweat of his brow, had accumulated more money than he had ever dreamed of, he had wanted to take his young wife to India. Not on a package tour, as was customary, but as individual travelers. They would take the plane from Roissy Charles-de-Gaulle airport, and after having flown over the roof of half the world they would arrive in a land that stretched over the horizon, here brown and bare, there green and humming with bird song, as warm and embracing as a mother, as recalcitrant as a young bride. In the city of Jaipur, the wind moans through the thousand windows of the palace.

But Rosa had made a face. All she could dream of was a winter in Paris, a lackluster city, which Sylvestre had visited twice. So India had crawled into that corner of his dreams that would never materialize.

Sylvestre had been an attentive papa for his boys, protective to

---

[25] An island dish made with curry.

[26] The festival of the dead.

[27] The festival of light.

the point that he had been worried to death about Carmélien until the boy had got back from Bordeaux and gone to live with Hosannah Taillefer, a câpresse, not in the least bit Indian—but times have changed from the days when Indians only married Indians, God works in mysterious ways; Sylvestre had been worried out of his mind about Jacques who, unlike his older brother, sowed his wild oats; he had tightened his control over Alain, who was basically lazy by nature, and pampered Alix who, by coincidence, had been born on his fortieth birthday. However, he had always considered Vilma as belonging to Rosa and had kept himself at a discreet distance from the circle of women. He had shown his love for her once by choosing her a husband, Marius Vindrex, the only son of his bosom friend, who had inherited some rich land up at Dillon from his mother, a Barthélemy, and owned the biggest sawmill in the area. For what matters in today's Guadeloupe is no longer the color of your skin—well, not entirely—nor an education. It was our fathers who worked themselves to the bone to be able to stick their fly-specked paper diplomas on their wooden walls. Nowadays, the high school graduates, master embroiderers of French French, sit on their doorsteps waiting for their unemployment checks. No, what matters is money, and Vilma would have money to spare. Marius had already bought land at Sainte-Anne and planned to build a studio residence for tourists, with private bathrooms.

Sylvestre had never understood why this child of his who never said anything but "Yes, Papa," with eyes lowered, had rebelled, taking up with a good-for-nothing stranger, half-mad and old enough to be her father. Who knows what goes on in that secret calabash of a young girl's head? Did she reproach him for taking her out of school? Had she decided to punish him by tarnishing his name?

Until Francis Sancher had seduced his daughter, Sylvestre

Ramsaran had never given him a second thought. He had other things on his mind! At the start of the year, a tropical depression had flattened his banana plantations. It was a crying shame! Tons of bananas down the drain, and as for any compensation, not a word from the préfet, Diablotin. Then a disease had attacked his experimental plantation of limes. New crops were as fragile and capricious as young girls and people were never tired of lamenting the good old days of sugarcane when, year in and year out, the oxcarts had trundled along to the factory, loaded to capacity. Sylvestre had been reluctant to change his ways. But you have to keep up with the times!

There was no denying the fact that the death of sugarcane was sounding the knell for something else in the country. What can we call it?

Sylvestre recalled how he used to hand out the pay to the workers for Rodrigue, calling each of them by their name, week after week:

"Louis Albert!"

"Louison Fils-Aimé!"

He remembered how he guided their stiff fingers, clumsily clutching the pen that scratched the register. How he snapped his whip over the head of the oxen as he drove the cart. Now everything was electronic and Carmélien was seriously talking of buying a computer for his crayfish business!

No, he really hadn't had time to waste thinking about Francis Sancher. One day, he had gone into Chez Christian, something he seldom did, disliking the bunch of drunks who had been holding up the counter since morning, and he had seen him leaning against the bar. Even though he was drunk at five in the afternoon, you could see immediately that here was a man of education and learning, who had nothing in common with the country louts around him. He was hollering out:

"I shall return each season with a chattering, green bird on my fist . . ."

And the men were laughing behind his back and pointedly touching their forehead. Not long after that Sylvestre had heard about Mira's rape and, devoid of compassion, had said to himself deep down that by hanging around in gullies she had reaped what she had sown. What a crying shame! Little did he know that the future would be even uglier and that his daughter, his own daughter . . . ! A wave of anger washed over him. What was he going to do with this papaless child who would soon open its eyes to the world? What was he going to do with Vilma's ruined youth?

He turned towards Vilma, who was plunged in tears, and his eyes met Rosa's, perpetually hostile, perpetually accusing, constantly contradicting his wife's docile behavior. In the name of Heaven! What could Rosa possibly reproach him for? Throughout their almost thirty years of life together, Sylvestre had only escaped their hardly hospitable bed once. Ah, Céleste Rigaud! To his dying day he would remember the smell of the sea from her thighs. Recalling this, his lips curled up in a smile and people exchanged meaningful looks of surprise. Was Sylvestre Ramsaran forgetting where he was and what was kicking in his daughter's belly?

Léocadie Timothée

That corpse is mine. It's no coincidence that I was the one to find him, already bloated, on the forest path at the time of day when the sky bleeds behind the mountain. I have become his mistress and his accomplice. I won't leave him until the first shovelfuls of earth fall on his wooden coffin.

And yet while he was alive there was no love lost between that man and me, and I was of the same opinion as those who were about to send a registered letter to the mayor asking for him to be expelled like the Haitians and the

Dominicans who turn the soccer fields in Petit-Bourg into cricket pitches. Really, this country is going to the dogs. It belongs to anybody now. French from France, all types of white folks from Canada or Italy, Vietnamese, and then this one comes and settles down in our midst, regurgitated by I don't know what bird of ill omen. I'm telling you, our country has changed. In times gone by, we knew nothing about the world and the world knew nothing about us. The fortunate few braved the sea to Martinique. Fort de France was on the other side of the world and everyone dreamed about gold in Guyana. Nowadays, there's not a single family who doesn't have one branch living in French France. People go off to visit Africa and America. The Indians go back to bathe in their river and the earth is as microscopic as a pinhead.

I was the first to open the one-room school here in Rivière au Sel. That was in 1920. I was twenty years old. At that time the Farjol factory still employed a thousand men, who lived in the sugarcane alleys scattered around the overseer's house, the only one where electricity switched on and off the light. All day long its chimneys spewed out columns of tar-colored smoke higher than the tallest mango trees and dirtied the sky. The air was heavy with the smell of cane trash and molasses. As black as their parents' poverty, my red-peppercorned-hair pupils would tie their shoes by their laces and carefully hang them around their necks. Since there wasn't any school canteen, they ate their midday meal of cassava flour and smoked herring under the covered playground. I had four rooms to myself, and since this was the first time I had left my maman's house and slept alone in a bed, far from the warmth of my sister's body, the horses of the night galloping until first light kept me awake with their whinnying and the sound of their hooves.

On Thursdays, I sank my heels in the sand along the beach at

Viard, studded with clams and chaubettes,[28] shellfish in mourning like a housewife's dirty nails. I didn't know how to swim. So I stayed far from the sea who called to me with the voice of a madwoman:

"Come nearer, nearer. Tear off your clothes. Plunge in. Let me roll over you, squeeze you and rub your body with my seaweed. Don't you know this is where you came from? Don't you know I'm part of you? Without me, you wouldn't be alive."

Once I came across a man and a woman making love under an almond tree. Not at all embarrassed, they shouted such obscenities I started to run. On Sundays I went to Mass at Petit-Bourg. The crowded church smelled of sweat, eau de Cologne and incense. On the square in front of the church, at a respectful distance from the tabernacle, the men would talk about the calamity of sugarcane, which was dying a natural death. Inside, the women would be praying to God in raptures and the choirboys, little devils in surplices, singing with their angelic voices. I would strike my breast in blue serge and sob the Agnus Dei for all the sins that others had committed for me.

Why did I choose to bury myself at twenty in this hole? Because I wanted to work for my race. My papa worked for the party founded by Monsieur Légitimus and was born in a one-story house next to the Légitimus family home on the island of Marie-Galante.

At the age of fifteen he had been forced to take up carpentry and consequently had been unable to study at the lycée Carnot and become a member of the "Young Sharks" with other underprivileged children like himself who wanted to turn their backs on their parents' destitution. Eventually he became Légitimus's right-hand man and galloped across Grande-Terre on horseback to

[28] Creole word for a cockle.

arouse the black man from his torpor. That's how he almost met his death in front of the inappropriately-named Bonne Mère factory. He had brought me up with his ideas.

But in Rivière au Sel the idea of race had a nasty taste to it. My pupils' parents could not understand why their children had to waste their time with me. They kept their boys home to water the oxen at the ponds, to tie the sugarcane during the harvesting season, and to kill the pig at Christmas. Their daughters were needed day and night.

When they passed me by, they grumbled words whose meaning I could guess from their expression and the furrows on their brow. It took me some time to understand the reason for their attitude. Our skins were the same color, our hair the same texture. And yet I was living in opulence, without hardship, in a house with a veranda and an attic. I had my fish cleaned by a maid who served me two meals a day. In their eyes I was a traitor! I suffered from this isolation because I wanted to be loved. I didn't know there's no love lost between black folks.

As the years went by my heart hardened. I took my revenge on the children. I had them kneel on both knees right in the middle of the school yard with the sun stuck like a cutlass between their shoulder blades and the sweat dripping salty down their foreheads. I had them recite multiplication tables until they were hoarse, copy out pages upon pages. I didn't let them out until darkness had set in, overjoyed at watching them shake with fright at the thought of Ti Sapoti or the Werewolf lunging out of the forest.

After five years a white school inspector came from France and exclaimed:

"Mademoiselle Léocadie! You've done miracles!"

And at the age of thirty-nine I became the head of a school with four classes. My maman wept for joy.

It was then my whole life changed. It was 1939. All around me people were saying the Germans were about to declare war on France. Some of them were stocking up with salted meat, some with codfish, others with wheat flour, sure that we were soon going to be short of everything. I had my own worries to think about. I was watching my youth fade away. How quickly it had gone! It had melted like a candle in front of the altar to the Virgin Mary, and all that was left was a warm little puddle of melted dreams. For a long time I had hoped a man would relieve me of the watch I kept up night and day over my solitude. And then that hope died as well.

When school went back in October, Déodat Timodent had been transferred to Rivière au Sel from Le Moule for disciplinary reasons. Everyone knew him because he had spoken out in *La Voix du Peuple* against the way history was being taught, recalling that the Gauls were not our ancestors. Now the administration was reprimanding him for much more serious misdemeanors. In a warehouse on the wharf he had got together with four of his closest friends, a shoemaker, a carpenter, an elementary school teacher and a doctor (this one was a mulatto), and discussed communism. At the time it was considered a dangerous, underground doctrine. Today, everyone's a Communist or in favor of independence.

Déodat Timodent had a reddish skin, was not very tall, not very big, not very elegant in his crumpled white drill suit, nothing very noticeable in appearance under his khaki-colored helmet. Yet when he laid his sparkling eyes on me, something was aroused in the shadowy depths of my body. He introduced himself respectfully and took possession of a small house not far from mine. Soon he got every tongue in Rivière au Sel wagging. Every Saturday, the sounds of the béguine, the mazurka and the polka could be heard from his little living room. Men and women came up from La Pointe and the night vibrated with laughter. I would curl up on my bed and try not to hear anything. On Sunday mornings, when I went down to Petit-Bourg, I passed in front of his door, shut tight on a heavy sleep that was more incriminating than the bacchanalia of the night before.

When I returned in the early afternoon, light-skinned girls in satin slips would be combing their curly hair, languidly rocking themselves back and forth. When Déodat Timodent was in my company, all he could give me was a solemn "Mademoiselle la Directrice." Wasn't I a woman in his eyes? Up till then I hadn't really paid attention either to the face or to the body the Good Lord had given me. I had been content with my intelligence that had taken me from my parents' rumshop to my position as elementary school teacher, then school principal. Yet I knew full well that all that didn't count for much in the eyes of Déodat Timodent.

One day, tired of all this respect, I planted myself in front of the mirror and examined myself.

What did I see?

A black-skinned woman whose oily skin was shiny from the heat. A face entirely eaten up by two sad yet eager eyes above hollow cheekbones and a mouth set tight as a boxfish's over thirty-two uneven, though very white, teeth. A thick mop of hair tracing the point of a widow's peak above a protruding forehead. A figure as flat as a pancake, nothing up front and nothing behind. Devoid of grace. Devoid of charm. That was me. Yes, that was my body. That was the prison I had been sentenced to live in. From that day on, I became embittered. I began to hold a grudge against the whole world and against my parents in particular, who believed that improving the race meant educating it and cramming its head with lessons on local history and geography. All I needed was a little loveliness. Or, failing that, a light skin which serves the same purpose where we come from.

My new frame of mind resulted in a longer list of punishments, but a higher success rate for the Certificate of Elementary Studies.

Déodat Timodent had been living in Rivière au Sel for four years, four years of suffering in silence. Are men blind to the love we show them? In any case, others could see it.

They saw it like the sun or the moon high in the sky and Rivière au Sel made up all sorts of jokes on the subject. In the evening the men would sit in front of their cabins strumming on their banjos while the women sang between sniggers: "Maladie d'amour, maladie de la jeunesse . . ."[29]

My servant girl, who was part of the plot, decked all the vases around the house with withered roses of unrequited love while my pupils wrote on the blackboard in red chalk: "Limbé, limbé."[30]

One Thursday I could take it no longer. I ran to the beach at Viard. That day the sea was nasty, angered by the icy wind that was whipping her shoulders.

"Listen to me carefully," she scolded, tossing her head of spray in every direction. "Why are you hoarding your hymen? Will you never know how much a man weighs, how he's even heavier after making love? Will you never whimper with cries of pleasure? If it's this Déodat you want, then go and take him!"

Filled with renewed energy, I returned to Rivière au Sel, the sweat of determination trickling down my back.

Déodat Timodent lived opposite what was to become the forestry house where Dodose and Emmanuel Pélagie now live with their unfortunate son. Pale pink hibiscus were growing in the garden and there was a bower of passion fruit. I pushed open the gate and swept onto the veranda like a hurricane that has picked up strength over the Atlantic and finally reached maximum speed.

---

[29] A popular song in the French Caribbean about being young and lovesick.

[30] A refrain from the same song.

Déodat rushed out. He was dressed in a small pair of yellow undershorts that gaped open, hinting at unknown depths, and I was able to admire this body, this male body that had been promised to me and to every woman since the morning of Creation, but which I had never taken possession of.

The biceps of his arms were bulging as if constantly at work, his pectoral muscles were thrown out above a flat torso, furrowed with a line of hair that thickened as it reached the narrow waist and pelvis, and above the superb, massive legs there was all that territory that for now was hidden from my gaze, although I could make out its softness as well as its firm and powerful curve. My head spun, I couldn't utter a word. It seemed I was about to pass out or faint from waiting. It was then that Déodat began to speak.

"I'm sorry, Mademoiselle la Directrice. I'll have finished my corrections by tomorrow. Tomorrow."

My eyes worked up his body to his face. His mouth was trembling, his eyes were terrified. He was scared. Yes, he was scared of me. I had come to offer myself with all my qualifications, my school with four classes and the academic honors the governor had awarded me the previous year, and he was scared. Misunderstanding my silence, he repeated:

"I promise, Mademoiselle la Directrice. Swear to God!"

All the words I had prepared dried up in my throat. My blood turned to ice. I could only show him my back to hide the salt water from my eyes and withdraw as quickly as I had come. Once I got home I threw myself onto the bed and started to cry. I cried from morning to evening. I didn't notice the night swoop down on Rivière au Sel like a bird of prey. It seemed that my life might just as well have stopped right there since Déodat Timodent would never be mine.

When I awoke the next morning, I looked at myself in the

mirror and saw myself even uglier, even blacker, together with an expression I had never seen before: a hard, mean look, shut tight as a prison door. I realized I had become another woman. Without love, a woman's heart hardens. It becomes a desolate savanna where only cacti grow. From that moment on even worse stories started to circulate about me. People said I cast kakwè.[31] They began to call me openly "vié volan"[32] and "old devil."

It was wartime, Governor Sorin's time. Since I owned a plot of land that the schoolchildren tended for me on Thursdays and Saturday afternoons, I didn't suffer too much. I had my own breadfruit, my yams, pigeon peas and Lima beans. A couple of rabbits gave me young ones. My hens laid eggs as big as a fist. For the rest, I got by, cutting out my dresses from French flour sacks and making my sandals from rubber tires. Oh no, I wasn't elegant! People had every reason to giggle behind my back, but I didn't mind.

One afternoon, it was a Tuesday, I shall remember it until the day I die, I was teaching my pupils to recite a poem that I had taken from *La Guadeloupe Pittoresque,* for I found it strange that the little Guadeloupeans are never taught anything about their own country:

> *"Guadeloupe! Ton ciel resplendit sur nos têtes*
> *De son bleu lumineux très doux et très profond;*
> *Comme un flot colossal qui monte à l'horizon*
> *Ta montagne est plus bleue encore dans tes crêtes."*[33]

---

[31] *Spells.*

[32] *Old witch.*

[33] *By Dominique Guesde. "Guadeloupe! Your sky shines over our heads/With its very soft and very deep blue light;/Like a colossal wave that sweeps up to the horizon/Your mountain is bluer still in its ridges."*

Suddenly I heard a commotion in the school recreation yard and a squadron of gendarmes turned up, arms at the ready. Dé-odat Timodent saw them too and rushed out of the classroom like a madman. Not fast enough! The gendarmes caught hold of him, put him in handcuffs and dragged him outside struggling and swearing under the sun.

It seems he had organized convoys to Dominica for those who wanted to join the Free French Forces and help General de Gaulle. Déodat Timodent wasn't liberated until Sorin had gone. People treated him like a hero. Since then he has gone into politics and has been a Communist deputy for two or three terms. I never saw him again.

And that's the only love story I can speak of.

Ever since, age has crept up on me in silence. The years have piled up. My heart and my body have forgotten they belonged to a living person and I have been content to cope with the thankless task of teaching. This modest little country school, painted in pink and green behind its narrow school yard planted with fine mango trees, whose fruit are catapulted down by impudent children during recreation, has produced a cardiologist, who is a credit to our race, and the principal of the lycée Gerville-Réache in Basse-Terre.

The Lameaulnes, and Loulou like the rest of them, have always refused to send their children here. They wouldn't dream of letting them learn to read and write next to some little nigger, a child from some wretched home. But believe me, if they had given me Mira I would have made someone out of her, because I know how to get blood out of a stone. She wouldn't be where she is today with no education or qualifications to bring up her papaless child. From what I hear, Loulou doesn't want to see the child and says the child will have to be put into care. If that isn't a shame! A child should always be considered the Good Lord's most beautiful gift!

Oh, he will have done some harm, this Francis Sancher, before setting off along the road to the Eternal Life.

I only saw him once while he was alive. That was quite enough! Every morning and every evening I take a walk to oil my old bones. The morning walk is shorter than the evening's. In the morning I get my body to go as far as the Lameaulnes Nurseries, sometimes making a detour by the forest path. I breathe in the dew, I watch a sleepy, lazy sun gather strength and climb up to sit in the sky; I gather wild verbena leaves for my evening tea. Sometimes I meet Mama Sonson, up like me by first light, and we have a chat.

That's how, one day, one morning, I met Francis Sancher. I had left the road where it continues straight between the casuarina trees, and walked into the undergrowth, after having skirted Pé Salvon's yellow yam field. Those yams were coming up a treat! Their leaves were shiny as if they had been varnished and their stalks twined gracefully around their poles.

Oh, I had heard about him inside out. But I had never seen him with my own two eyes, this man who was turning Rivière au Sel upside down. A well-built, brown-skinned mulatto, whose hair was too gray for such a young-looking face, was sitting on a tree trunk at the entrance to the forest path, and seemed to be far, far away from the land of the living. I stepped forward out of curiosity to take a closer look and get a sense of him for myself when my foot slipped and three rocks rolled loose and ended up against a tree stump. At the sound, he looked up, saw me and stood up while a crazed terror distorted his face as he stared wide-eyed and openmouthed. He was afraid. Of me. I was about to shout:

"My name's Léocadie Timothée. I live at the crossroads near the top of the hill."

But he had started to run and he ran until he disappeared into the darkness between the trees, and I remained standing there, my hand on my mouth recalling the forgotten taste of old sufferings. It's true. I had forgotten I was a scarecrow that sent men, love and happiness running. They would never settle on my branches. I went home, barricaded my solitude and cried every tear out of my body. I cried as I had never cried for fifty years. I realized that my heart had remained a fragile, ever so fragile bulb, wrapped in layers of skin that I thought were tough, but in fact were easily sliced by the knife of suffering.

I never saw Francis Sancher again. I heard he was continuing his mischief and he had set his sights on the innocent Vilma, the baby I had seen swell Rosa's womb month after month, Rosa who never stopped lamenting for her little Shireen, dead a few months earlier. Vilma came into our joyless world one June morning while Sylvestre had gone to buy some bulls in Le Moule, which meant that he only saw his daughter when she was two days old. I won't make any secret about it, I wished nothing good on that man who had come to plant misfortune among us, and I do believe that for once the Good Lord heard me. Try as I may I can't pretend I feel anything else. Only that selfish feeling the sight of a corpse gives you: the fear of what tomorrow will bring us. For two cents I'd change places and go and sit in the other room or on the veranda with those who don't care about pretenses, who keep an eye on the rum bottles and finish their plates of thick soup as they listen to Cyrille the storyteller shout his "yé krik" and his "yé krak."[34]

---

[34] *The traditional opening by the storyteller in Creole.*

Cyrille the Storyteller

"Yé krik, yé krak!

"Ladies and gentlemen, a good evening to you; a very good evening to you. A good evening to one and all! The person you see in front of you, looking like a bwa bwa[35] that's paraded through the streets of La Pointe during carnival, is no ordinary nigger. That's what you were thinking, weren't you? You were saying to yourself, Cyrille is not far off fifty and all he has to his name under the sun is a house

---

[35] *A marionette.*

made of breeze blocks, and it's not even painted. The gutter's broken and, when it pours, the water overflows from the roof, plop, plop, plop. But let me tell you, when I was twenty I was tired of kicking my heels against the hills and mountains of this tiny scrap of land and I said: 'Fare thee well!' I left for Marseille. There I took a boat that was waiting in the harbor and here I was tossing and reeling on the sea until we reached . . . until we reached Dakar. In Africa. Yes, Africa. And what did I see, ladies and gentlemen? Not at all what I had been told. There were no naked niggers eating each other up. No! There were Mercedes-Benz! Did you know that? How many are there on our roads? There were flags, their very own in yellow, red and green. Presidential palaces with presidents in tails. Whores dressed in silk and lamé cooing: 'Like a good time, darling?' Oh, Lord! I would have stayed on in Africa if the Africans hadn't given me a big kick in the ass and shouted: 'Go back where you came from!' And here I am in front of you to tell you the tale I just had time to hear from them. 'One day the hyena, the monkey and the lion . . .' "

Standing under the tarpaulin that let in the rain, Cyrille was doing his usual antics and everyone was guffawing. Yet his heart wasn't in it. When Alix Ramsaran had found him with both feet in his yam patch and announced that Francis Sancher had passed on and that he was needed at the wake, he had been flabbergasted. Only a few days earlier, less than a week in fact, he had come across Francis Sancher sitting on a tree trunk. It had been early morning, along the Saint-Charles forest path. Since he didn't indulge in the gossip of Rivière au Sel and cared little about how many girls' bellies had been made to swell up by Francis Sancher, he had greeted him politely.

"Sa ou fè?"

Francis Sancher had made a face, as if colic had tied a knot in his guts at that very moment, and motioned him to sit down next to him. Cyrille had obeyed, again out of politeness, and Francis Sancher had pulled a bottle of rum from Marie-Galante out of a bag, the very kind that bowls you over if your head isn't screwed on tight to both shoulders. Cyrille had declined the offer. He was not one of those who start drinking as soon as their eyes are open, and Francis Sancher had pointed to the Soufrière, serene and well-behaved, with a gray veil knotted around its neck, and said:

"I wish it would erupt, that volcano! Set the whole place alight so I wouldn't be the only one to go!"

Somewhat surprised, Cyrille had remarked:

"It's a good volcano, there's no denying that! The last time it got angry was in 1976. That's over ten years ago. But what frightened us, really frightened us, was in 1956. I had just reached twenty. So I wasn't thinking about death. One morning I opened my eyes and everything was black. A cloud of ashes had fallen on the flowers, the leaves, the animals tied up in the savanna, and the rivers heaved in mourning. Oh, it was no joke, that time!"

Francis Sancher looked around him.

"You know, it looks remarkably like home, this little corner!"

Cyrille couldn't help being curious (there's no sin in that), and had let out:

"Home is Cuba, from what I hear?"

But Francis Sancher had shaken his head.

"No, Cuba is the country I chose for my rebirth. You see, I was naïve about that. It's impossible. You are never born again. You never come out twice from your mother's womb. You can't tell her: 'It didn't work, take me back!' Once you're up on your two feet, you have to go on to the end, right to the grave. I've walked until I'm exhausted! The marathon started a long time ago. It seems that my great-grandfather, a certain François Désiré, the first of this sinister lineage I want to end with me, was a Frenchman, the son of a wealthy family, who, after committing the first of his crimes, had crossed the sea and settled these islands with his vileness."

Dizzy from all this verbiage and determined to demonstrate he could be just as masterful with words, Cyrille managed to get in:

"Let me tell you that from the first, the very first crossing my family has never left this patch of land. They've remained stuck in the ground like a rock. They've never even gone as far as that island as flat as your hand you can see over there on a fine day, the island of Marie-Galante! The farthest I've ever been is Deshaies on the other side. They called me in to sit up with Zéphyr, a master storyteller, who, between you and me, was too fond of the bottle. Don't think I underestimate the powers of rum! It has to flow for the candles to shine and the women with watery eyes to pray. Our grandfathers used to say: 'Si pa ti ni wom, pa ti ni lapwyè.' (No rum, no prayer.) Do you hear what I'm saying? But too much is too much. And one day Zéphyr collapsed in his field. Dead."

Francis Sancher had taken advantage of the moment when Cyrille let the word "dead" swell up in the silence to resume talking.

"It's funny, isn't it? Now that my time has come I'd readily plead for a few more days, a few more weeks, a few more months. The bitch hasn't left me alone for a single minute. She's waltzed me round and round without music, and yet now I'd willingly go on under her iron rule. Alas, there's nothing to be done. I have only a few days left."

A few days?

At the time Cyrille hadn't paid much attention to these words. If anybody was bursting with health, it was Francis Sancher, with his bakoua[36] stuck on his head right down to his eyes and his well-ironed clothes bursting at the seams, which proved he had a

---

[36] *Traditional French Caribbean hat.*

woman back at the house. Moreover, he had very quickly forgotten about him. He had met Xantippe with his mask of a face pretending to look for rabbit food, and he had told himself deep down that an eye would have to be kept on this vagabond, who was supposed to be harmless, but whose look gave you the creeps. Thank goodness Rivière au Sel had been spared those crimes that were common in the rest of the country: robbery, rape and murder! What were we coming to? Hadn't he read in his daily copy of *France-Antilles* that three teenagers had held up a gas station in Le Moule? Back home he had had to deal with Sandra, his wife, who had started to prattle on because he had taken all this time to pick a few miserable taro leaves.

Yet when Alix had come to fetch him, he had recalled this meeting a few days earlier, realizing that this talkative and undeniably energetic man was waiting for his death. And that perhaps he had been the last person to see him alive, since Mademoiselle Timothée Léocadie had stumbled on his body at the end of this forest path, close to a small bamboo grove that the catchers of crayfish used to ransack but was now growing thick and healthy.

Yes, he had been waiting for his death, seated on a moss-covered tree stump, with a steady stream of soldier ants feverishly busying themselves between his feet. How had he met his death? Had he heard her step crush the damp grass? Had she loomed up unexpected out of the heliconias? Had she leaned against a wild cherry tree and warned him of her presence with the dry cough of a Gitane smoker?

Cyrille the storyteller, whose reputation was firmly established and much in demand from Petit-Bourg to Vieux Habitants, had seen some corpses in his lifetime! Fat ones, skin-and-bones ones, short ones, tall ones, red ones, black-black ones, almost white ones, Indian ones, all equal once they were cold and stiff. Yet he had never come face to face with death herself. He imagined her as a

Negress with pearly-white teeth sparkling between her thick lips, the color of black beauty aubergine, swaying her hips seductively, stirring up a fire in the loins. Or else like Mira, a scorching high yellow girl who would set a church font on fire.

For if she was as ugly as sin, with an ugly grin and a scythe over her shoulder, why would everybody want to follow her? Everybody without exception. Francis Sancher was waiting for her. And perhaps if he had hung around he would have seen her too and they would have found two bodies in the mud. At the thought of this Cyrille's teeth started to chatter and he began to stammer:

"Once-upon-a-time-there-was-a-pretty-girl-who-said-that-she-wouldn't-marry-any-man-who-had-the-slightest-mark-I-mean-scar-on-his-body."

Amazed, the audience looked at each other. What had come over their favorite storyteller to mistalk like that?

Rosa, Vilma's Mother

Cyrille the storyteller talks and talks and his story reminds me of another one my maman used to tell me during the long September rains when the clouds would fly black and low on the horizon like birds of prey.

"In Matouba, a mother had a daughter who was the apple of her eye. The girl was lovely, very lovely; her mouth was a pink and mauve Jamaican plum; her eyes like two stars out of the firmament. She didn't want to marry anyone. People came up from Grande-Terre loaded with flowers, fruit and root vegetables to ask for her hand. She acted hard to please, turned up her nose, shook her hair in every direction and went up and locked herself in her room. One day while she was at the attic window, drinking in the cool air that came down from the volcano, she saw a tall, handsome man with a gun slung over his shoulder arrive on a dapple gray horse. She looked and she looked and then went downstairs to find her maman.

" 'Mother dear, mother dear, I've seen the man I want to marry.'

"Her maman shook her head and said: 'Pitite an mwen (my child), beware! There's nothing good about men. You don't know this man from Adam and he might even be a guiab (a devil). He'll eat you up.'

"Her daughter refused to listen . . ."

I, Rosa Ramsaran, I'm not afraid to say that all men are guiabs. There's no exception to the rule.

When they married me off to Sylvestre Ramsaran, nobody asked for my opinion. I was living happily in my parents' house. My father's cattle grazed in tightly-packed herds on his land in the Grands-Fonds, lowing intermittently like the sound of the conch and lifting their black muzzles skyward. On Sundays my sisters and I would tie blue taffeta ribbons in our braids. One day, father called me.

"Sylvestre Ramsaran is coming for a meal. He's a good fellow, you'll see. You'll live in Rivière au Sel. It's a long way, over on Basse-Terre. But he'll bring you to see us every month and you'll also spend each Christmas here."

Sylvestre Ramsaran arrived at twelve on the dot, a trilby hat on his head, wearing sneakers and looking very pleased with himself.

I said to Gina, my sister:

"Never, I'll never marry that man!"

"It's all the books you read that have gone to your head," Gina retorted. "And besides, what's so wonderful about living amid the

smell of cow dung? If I could leave in your place I would! They
say he's loaded with money, even more than Father, and that he
goes to French France all the time."

Father gave me an expensive wedding because I was the first
daughter to leave home. I went to Puerto Rico to buy my pure lace
wedding dress and my low, white satin shoes. Bottle upon bottle of
Veuve-Clicquot flowed freely, but my tears flowed faster than the
champagne. Around 10 p.m. Sylvestre and myself left for Rivière
au Sel. Sylvestre didn't speak to me. At every corner he would
sing:

> "Amantine, Amantine ro
> Rouvè la pot ban mwen
> La pli ka mouyé mwen."[37]

When we got to Rivière au Sel it was dark. Street lamps that
looked as though they were hanging from the thick vegetation lit
up patches of the road. You could make out the lighted dots of the
cabins.

Sylvestre hurt me. He tore me.

When the sun had risen, I ran out onto the veranda and was
suffocated by what I saw. A dark green tangled mass of trees,
creepers and parasites, broken here and there by the lighter green
of the banana groves. Watching over it all was the formidable
mountain. I thought in my heart:

"Oh, God, is this where I'm going to live!"

In the Grands-Fonds, where our family comes from, the land is
as flat as the back of your hand. The waves of sugarcane reach to
the horizon. Voices are carried on the wings of the wind.

Yet, gradually, to my heart's surprise, I grew to love Rivière au

---

[37] Amantine, Amantine, oh,/Open the door/The rain is soaking me.

Sel. A kind of call goes up from the surrounding forest. Climbing the Saint-Charles forest path I would strike off into the depths of the woods, wandering between the columns of trees that held high their crested heads. I would sit between their roots and stay there for hours on end.

Soon, however, I had no time left for that, because I had two sons, Carmélien and Jacques, one after the other, by Sylvestre.

"The iron rod's[38] working well," he would repeat, so proud of his boys.

I too was proud at first. When the midwife exclaimed: "Sé an ti-gason, oui!" (It's a boy!) my heart thumped against my breast. But I hadn't reckoned on Sylvestre's behavior. As soon as the boys could lift up their little heads he would take them everywhere he went.

"Hey, Sylvestre!" people would call out. "Aren't you forgetting it wasn't your belly that carried the boys? A man's not a woman!"

But he would ignore them or else answer back:

"Tell me about it."

Sometimes he even took them along when he went hunting thrushes or woodpigeons, and I prayed to the Good Lord my children wouldn't come back to me with a hole in their heads. But the older they got, the further they grew away from me. Not only did Sylvestre take them away from me but so did school. My heart was drained.

One Sunday while we were having lunch in the Grands-Fonds, I left the men to discuss the slump in the price of bananas and went and joined my mother in the kitchen. She was arranging the fruit salad in dishes with her lovely hands dappled with veins. She listened to me absentmindedly.

"You have the best of husbands and you're complaining! Does

---

[38] *The male sex.*

he chase other women? Does he beat you? What you're telling me is perfectly normal. Boys are made to be with their papa. If you want someone all to yourself, have a little girl."

A few weeks later I missed my blood and I realized I was pregnant. But once again it was a boy, my third, Alain, and the same thing started up all over again. As soon as Alain could stand on his own two feet, Sylvestre took him for himself. He would take him into the forest and name the trees for him: châtaignier, medicine tree and so on. Out of despair I went to see Mama Sonson. It is said in Rivière au Sel that Mama Sonson can do anything. People even come from far and wide to consult her. It's thanks to her that Wilfred has remained with his wife, when his heart had already left for Saint-Sauveur with Rose Aimée. It's thanks to her that Larose is elected mayor of Petit-Bourg year after year, and nobody else ever will be, neither a Communist nor an RPR.[39] It was Mama Sonson too who made George's male member soft and powerless because Eulalie was tired, so tired of all those illegitimate children he was bringing into the house.

When I went to see her, Mama Sonson was amazed.

"Well, it's the first time someone has asked me something like that!" she cried out. "Boys! All they want is boys to keep their man. You, you want a daughter? Is that what you want? I can't believe my ears!"

Then she gave me leaves to put in my bath water and potions to drink.

"Pray, pray to the Good Lord," she urged. "Don't stop praying, because He alone decides. People don't realize that my powers are governed by His will."

A year passed, then once again I missed my blood. But this time, I knew it was a girl from the very first weeks. By the delicate

---

[39] A French political party, right of center.

way she swam in my waters. By the very soft whisper of her voice. When evening fell we would chatter until the glimmer of first light, and she would tell me:

"Be patient. Soon I shall be in your arms. Curled up against your breast, gorging myself on your delicious white milk. As I grow up I shall bring you consolation every time you prick yourself on the thorns of life."

One night I had a dream. I found myself in India, our country of origin about which, alas, we no longer know very much. I was in a village with houses built of dried cow dung. In a courtyard some women were putting a baby into my arms whose face was wrapped in very fine white linen, and they were saying to me: "Here is Shireen."

The next day I gave birth. I didn't even feel any pain. The baby simply found its own way and slipped between my thighs, not covered with blood and fecal matter like the others, but clean and dry with silky skin! The midwife put her into my arms, exclaiming:

"What a lovely baby the Good Lord has given you!"

And she really was lovely.

Light-skinned, not black-black like Sylvestre and his boys. Eyes the color of smoke. Lips as pink as hibiscus buds.

"Shireen?" Sylvestre shouted. "What sort of a name is that?"

For once I stood my ground, and it was as Shireen that she came out of the church in her lace dress that swept the floor. Everyone was amazed. They couldn't understand why I was making such a fuss about a little girl whereas I had already been blessed with three boys.

How can I describe the happiness a child can give? However much the people from the post-natal clinic repeated at each session: "Be careful, Madame Ramsaran. She's not gaining enough weight," I preferred her to the three baby bulldogs I'd already given birth to. I watched her sleep in her cradle in a cloud of tulle, her arms joined above her head like a dancer's. I watched her distort her flower bud of a mouth into a yawn. I watched her breathe.

I watched her live. I had all I needed. I no longer felt Sylvestre climb on top of me and dig his knees into my thighs, then soak me with his liqueur. This happiness lasted three months, three months during which I was overcome with joy and thanked the Good Lord.

Then, one evening, I was in bed, I heard a thick, cavernous cough, a cough that signaled nothing good, coming from the other side of the wall in the room where she slept. I rushed in, and there she was with her eyes wide open, no longer sparkling with life, but dull as an animal's in its death throes, her mouth swarming with whitish worms. Her heart had already stopped beating.

I wanted to die, but I couldn't. I kept my eyelids shut tight, so tight, for the darkness to enter all of me as well.

I asked myself, why, oh why was the Good Lord punishing me in this way. I couldn't understand.

As for Sylvestre, he merely repeated: "Everyone could see she hadn't come to stay. She was as thin as a guava stick. I'll give you another little girl."

And he kept his word. After a few weeks I felt another child moving in the darkness of my womb. But I didn't want his daughter. I wanted to expel it before it was due. But I felt it clutching to my inside, a voracious parasite, feeding off my flesh and blood. I had to bear my cross to the very end, for nine interminable months, until she emerged, just like her father and her brothers, so different from my Shireen.

The heart does not accept orders.

I bore a grudge against her for living while my beloved Shireen had gone. For growing up and getting bigger while her sister was nothing but a wretched pile of little bones at the bottom of a box. I am guilty, I am the one to blame for all this unhappiness. For you don't need to look very far; a child's misfortunes can always be traced to the parents.

Yes, when that incredible thing happened to us, when Vilma, Vilma who never got her head out of a book, went and set up house with that man, I felt that something wasn't natural; I could feel the Good Lord starting to put his revenge in motion to crush and confound me. I wanted to confide in someone. But whom? Who would have listened to me? I carried my secret in solitude. Around me the men were making decisions, talking of killing her, of killing him. In the end, they didn't kill anyone. They went to negotiate with Francis Sancher. They didn't tell me anything about it, for, according to them, this was men's business that was settled between men.

When they came back with long faces, they didn't tell me anything either. I understood immediately though that their visit had served no purpose at all. They got together on the veranda, and I could hear Carmélien, as hotheaded as ever since he was back from French France where the white folks had treated him so badly, talking again of sharpening his machete and going to lie in wait for him along the Saint-Charles forest path.

"Go on!" I shouted. "If it's killing you want, finish me off. Don't you think we've got enough misery!"

They kept their voices down, but I knew. I knew they were talking revenge.

For three months I stayed put, working myself up into a state, with that remorse still gnawing at my heart. Lying beside Sylvestre, who never gives up, and night after night takes his pleasure, despite the years creeping up on all of us, I would repeat to myself: "It's my fault. I'm to blame for what's happening."

Then one morning when Sylvestre, Carmélien and Jacques had gone down to La Pointe in the Toyota, and Alix and Alain were at school, I made up my mind. I remember the bougainvillea were bleeding their blood over the orange plumes of the birds of paradise, I remember the sea between the trees was turquoise green, calm and peaceful. I remember it was a beautiful day.

Regardless of the pain that confines her to a rocking chair in front of the television, Madame Mondésir came out onto the veranda to spy on me. I passed her by, head up, with merely a "How are you feeling in yourself this morning?"

I didn't listen to her litany of moans and went on my way.

I'd heard a lot about Francis Sancher's dogs, but I had never seen them with my own two eyes. Black as coal with red patches on their feet, as if Hell had spewed them up on this earth still bearing its fiery traces. On seeing me they started to bark like the damned. Francis Sancher came out.

"Don't be frightened," he said. "They're the gentlest creatures on earth."

As I didn't move, he came forward and took them by the collar. Anybody who says that man is wicked, a public menace, can't have looked him in the eyes. His eyes are the color of the sand on the beach at Viard when the tide goes out leaving behind luminous little shells. They tell a story, a very sad and bitter story. Even though I am forty-five, how I would have liked to sit in a rocking chair and listen to him for hours on end, evening after evening, while the shadows enfolded us!

With an emotion in my voice that I had never felt before, I said:

"I'm Vilma's maman."

"She has your good looks," he replied.

I was amazed. Nobody had ever commented on my good looks before, and I don't think Vilma is particularly good-looking. Black-black like Sylvestre. What I liked was her hair, her braids that grew longer every day between my hands. Alas, when she was fourteen she went down to Beauté-Coiffure in Petit-Bourg, and without even asking me had them cut off.

"Where is she?" I asked. "I'd like to speak to her."

He smiled.

"Sit down. She won't be long."

He brought me a glass of water, which was probably all there was in the house, but it was cool and fragrant. He sat down not far from me on a whitewood chair, and after a while said:

"My mother must have white hair by now, whereas when I knew her it was black and shiny like yours. She never did love me very much. Never mind, she's my mother, the only one I'll ever have!"

"Why do you say that?" I stammered. "A mother can't help but love her children."

He shrugged his shoulders.

"It would be too easy. My father, you see, only married my mother because she was the daughter of one of the richest cafeiteros.[40] With all due respect, I'm sure he made love to her without even speaking to her. Difficult to love children born under those conditions. In order to be able to love, you have to have received a lot, a lot in return!"

That was me he was describing!

"How do you know that?" I exclaimed.

"From the time I was called 'curandero' I realized that the

---

[40] *A coffee planter.*

heart and the mind took precedence over everything else and that the body merely obeys."

I nodded in approval. It was sweet, so sweet to talk about myself that I couldn't stop.

"How true! Life's problems are like trees. We see the trunk, we see the branches and the leaves. But we can't see the roots, hidden deep down under the ground. And yet it's their shape and nature and how far they dig into the slimy humus to search for water that we need to know. Then perhaps we would understand."

He sighed.

"Nobody ever understands, Madame Ramsaran. Everyone is afraid of understanding. Take me, for instance. As soon as I tried to understand, to ask for an explanation for all those corpses, all that blood, they called me every name under the sun. As soon as I refused to go along with the slogans, they kept a serious eye on me. Nothing is more dangerous than a man who tries to understand."

"I would say you are a man of great wisdom!" I murmured.
He smiled.

"Wisdom? I wouldn't say that. Rather that I tried to untangle the skeins of life."

"Tell me about it."

There we were chatting on terms so intimate for the first time in my life, with things I wanted to say swirling around in my head, when Vilma arrived. When she saw me, she screamed:

"Go away! Go away! What are you doing here?"

He tried to intervene, but I was already outside.

I ran into the undergrowth until I was out of breath, and at one point my body refused to go on and felt so weak that I sat down on the root of a tree. Water streamed down my cheeks.

"In order to be able to love, you have to have received a lot, a lot in return," he had said.

I had never received any. My hands were empty. All I had ever done was serve.

After an hour I felt the weight of a presence, I looked up and saw Xantippe standing dead upright under a pink poui. When he noticed that I was watching him, he turned his back on me and slipped into the heart of the forest. I stayed sitting a good while longer and then got up.

Now Francis Sancher is dead. But he alone has come to an end. The rest of us are alive and continue to live as we've always done. Without getting along together. Without liking ourselves. Without sharing anything. The night is waging war and grappling with the shutters. Soon, however, it will have to surrender to the day and every rooster from every henhouse will crow its defeat. The banana trees, the cabins and the slopes of the mountain will gradually float to the surface of the shadows and prepare to confront the dazzling light of day. We shall greet the new face of tomorrow and I shall say to this daughter of mine:

"I gave birth to you, but I misloved you. I neglected to help you flower and you grew stunted. It's not too late for our eyes to meet and our hands to touch. Give me your forgiveness."

Carmélien

"I can't hide the fact that I hated him more for what he did to Mira than for what he did to my own sister Vilma."

The driving rain soaked the neck and shoulders of Carmélien, who didn't move a muscle but merely pulled an already wet handkerchief out of his pocket and instinctively wiped his skin and clothes with it. He liked the rain. He liked the feel of water. He particularly liked its smell when it rained

warm from the clouds; when you came across it unexpectedly
while rounding a patch of land that had been warmed to boiling
point by the midday sun; when it lay dormant, brown and brackish with grass and leeches; when it grew angry and rushed down
from the hills, churning the corpses of animals foolishly gone
astray. When he was little, out with Sylvestre, sometimes it would
come upon them without warning except for a sudden darkness in
the air and a heavy pattering on the foliage in the hills. While his
father ran for shelter under the banana trees, he would remain
standing in the middle of the field, lifting his little face up to the
sky that often stayed blue, closing his eyes, and opening his mouth
like the frogs and the toads probably did as they hid in the tall
grass. He must have developed this liking for water during his
baptism when the vatialou[41] had dipped him in the river three
times before shaving his head. Yes, it must have been then that he
recalled being back in the womb when, without eyes and with fins
for feet, he swam in happiness. During the rainy season, Rosa,
who gave up trying to understand him or to keep him locked up
within four walls, would sigh in a resigned tone of voice:

"Go and catch your death of cold, if that's what you want."

He would take off his clothes like those urchins he was forbidden to play with, whose papas were too busy burning their throats
with rum and whose mamans too busy spying on the neighbors.
He would stand motionless or else do somersaults and acrobatics.

When he was in the last grade of elementary school his teacher
had made them buy *Masters of the Dew*. For a boy who didn't like
reading, it was a revelation, and he wondered whether the story
hadn't been written just for him.

"He took her hand. 'Come!' He pushed the vines aside. She
walked in the mysterious shade of the giant fig tree.

---

[41] *Priest.*

" 'That's the keeper of the water,' she whispered in a sort of sacred terror. 'He's the keeper of the water.'

"She looked at the branches laden with silvery, floating moss.

" 'He's terribly old!'

" 'He's terribly old.'

" 'You can't see his head.'

" 'His head's in the sky.'

" 'His roots are like feet.'

" 'They hold the water.'

" 'Show me the water, Manuel.' "

So he too got it into his head to discover a new spring, and by trampling through the undergrowth, darting along the forest paths and stumbling over the buttress roots, he found one, above the Saint-Charles forest path. It bubbled out of the leaf mold between the ferns and the lichens, wound its way secretly before losing itself in the earth again, then reemerged a quarter of a mile farther on, strengthened and swollen by other underground springs. Armed with one of Sylvestre's machetes, he tried to unearth it where it hid in the ground and hollow out a bed for it to sprawl in splendor. Every afternoon, when school was out, Sylvestre would call to him in vain to take the oxen to the pond or light wood fires at the edge of the fields; Carmélien would be running towards the spring, his heart thumping like a lover running to his betrothed, and he would work hard until night fell. When he got back home, Rosa would snatch the stickweed from his hair, sniffing his smelly sweat and complaining:

"What have I done to the Good Lord to deserve a ragamuffin like you? And your father doesn't even say a word!"

At night he dreamed he too was master of the water, irrigating the grateful soil, ordering the pumpkins and eggplants to grow, and he would wake up in surprise in a pool of urine that would bring down Rosa's wrath in the morning, so that he would try to make up his bed on the sly.

One day, a thousand clues whispered to him that he was not the only one paying homage to his spring. Here the moss had been trampled on, there some ferns pulled up. Rocks had been wedged in the loose soil to form a bed. He had been stricken with rage, and had gone up earlier than usual to hide behind a mastwood tree to wait for the intruder, the enemy. After three afternoons of lying in wait, he saw a young girl emerge from the shadow of the thickets, as stealthy and agile as a thieving mongoose about to enter a henhouse, crowned with a mop of frizzy, golden hair, like a pagan halo around her face. It was Mira!

Like all those who lived in Rivière au Sel, Carmélien knew and respected the Lameaulnes, because they were almost white, because they lived in a house with "Private" written on the gate from which you could see nothing except for a brick-red roof between the fronds of the cabbage palms if you perched on the branches of a mango tree on the edge of the road; because they had so much money, said Sylvestre, who was a connoisseur of well-stocked bank accounts, they could have bought the whole of La Pointe if they wanted to. He had never paid much attention to Mira, even if he did hear Rosa and her friends savor every detail of the ravages she was causing, when they got together in the kitchen to shell the pigeon peas or string the beans; and so he vaguely knew that a mamaless child was the devil in person. He had, therefore, stayed put in his hiding place, wondering what attitude to take when, after a quick glance around her, Mira removed her clothes and splashed herself with water from head to foot.

At the age of thirteen, Carmélien was not one of those precocious scamps who gazed in admiration at the nudes in *Playboy* behind their half-open desks. He had no desire whatsoever to penetrate the mystery of the female body, and watched Rosa uncover her beautiful breast to feed Alix without batting an eye. Likewise, what she did at night with Sylvestre in the big bed carefully made up with a white sheet and two salmon-pink cushions at the head, that she had cross-stitched with red, yellow and green blue-finned fish the previous year when she was expecting Alix and the doctor had advised her to rest—what she did with Sylvestre didn't bother him at all. And yet when he saw Mira naked, with the light enveloping her in a yellow halo paler than her skin, which looked as if it had been cooked over and over again by the sun, he realized that unknowingly he had been blessed with manhood.

Lying motionless, face down on the ground while the water surged around the obstacle of her body before washing over it, Mira splashed herself, then rolled every which way. Suddenly, as if at a signal, she got up, collected her clothes and ran off. How little meaning there is to the Paradise of Childhood Love.

From one day to the next, Papa's boy, Carmélien—the boy whose papa gave him everything he wanted, even his very own shiny moped after having perched him for years on the handlebars of his bicycle, the boy who ignored the constant reprimands of his mother, paying as much attention to her babble as to the buzz of flies when the mango trees are in flower—Carmélien changed. He became a soul suffering in Hell, a zombie famished for salt. Monsieur Gervaise the History teacher found him crying hot tears in the toilets. Monsieur Dolomius the French teacher, who was so happy an Indian had made it to the top five in the class, thereby demolishing any remaining foolish prejudice, had gone up to see Sylvestre, and Sylvestre had been so worried he had taken his son to see his cousin Ramgoulam, a doctor at La Pointe d'Or. Scarcely had he taken a look at Carmélien than he cried out:

"It's puberty, for God's sake! You're so busy making money, Sylvestre, that you've forgotten how you felt at his age. Let me tell you, people say you've got a numbered bank account in Switzerland."

After this visit, Rosa had him drink a syrup of potassium gluconate morning and night, and Carmélien vomited from grief and nausea, once he had passed the hedge of rayo surrounding the house.

It seemed to him that this purgatory lasted for years (but it's common knowledge that grief drags time out), when fate in person decided to take a hand. It was August 15, Petit-Bourg's feast day. The sun had risen, all glowing and pleased with itself. The sky was blue with promises that were going to be kept. Carmélien, wearing a tie, and his brother Jacques had been going round the stands since morning with a crisp one-hundred-franc note in his pocket, when, in front of the lucky dip, he had seen Mira. A very different Mira from the little savage who day after day took her dubious pleasure stripping and rolling in the water. A Mira in a lace dress with buckles on her shoes, standing aloof from the others, watching the crowds with the sagacious look of a grown-up who was not impressed. Carmélien spun round, sweeping the vicinity with his gaze. No doubt about it! She was alone, and the troublesome silhouettes of her brothers, her zealous bodyguards, were nowhere to be seen. After a few minutes she set off in the direction of a shooting gallery, gave up trying to win a Creole doll, entered a dark room where a French French magician was reading the future, came out, looked down her nose at the dancers in the Touloulou ballet who, with hands on hips, were getting ready for a quadrille as doudou as you could get, and made straight for the gwo-ka drummers. It was then that Carmélien had an idea. Leaving Jacques standing on the spot, he ran to the souvenir stand and, laying down his crisp note on the table, took possession of the biggest Creole doll, the one that had everything: the pleated madras head-tie, the dangly earrings, the gold-beaded necklace, the heavy slave bracelet, the lace petticoat and the embroidered felt slippers.

With that mocking, scornful look common to all the Lameaulnes for generations, Mira was standing back from the crowd which was swaying and beating its hands in rhythm, for the gwoka has an irresistible effect on some! Carmélien went up to her, but what he didn't know was that love has powers over the vocal cords and can turn a first prize in recitation into a belching stammerer.

"It's for you!"

She seemed surprised, looked at the doll, then looked at him, from the flimsy shoes that Rosa had bought at Bata to the part Rosa had combed with Vitapointe brilliantine and splashed with Eau de Cologne Bien-Etre, and said quite simply:

"Kouli malaba!"[42]

Then she spun round on her heels.

Fifteen years later, Carmélien's pain was still intact, for the wounds of childhood do not heal. From that day on, he lost his taste for everything. It seemed he had never loved nor desired anyone else. In Bordeaux, people would take him for an Indian from India and talk to him about Satyajit Ray, of whom he had never seen a single film. He had nothing to say in reply, not only out of ignorance, but because he couldn't get Mira out of his head. When it came to making love he would see her again, his pain capturing her like a camera, mocking him in her lace dress with the Claudine collar and tiny mother-of-pearl buttons. So his male member would wither, and he would make for the door stammering apologies.

Ah, those years of study had been somber ones, and he'd soon lost his illusions about French France! Solitude. Drabness. He had

---

[42] *Indian from the Malabar coast. A common term of abuse.*

discovered he had a weak point: the sight of blood! During his internships at the hospital he had been filled with an immense terror at the sight of all that twisted, tortured and mutilated flesh, and was so upset he imagined he saw Mira in every patient. One summer he got it into his head to travel through Europe and had gone with some friends to Barcelona. The ocher façades and pink oleanders along the Ramblas did make a certain impression on him, and he could easily have lazed under the sun if his friends hadn't dragged him to a corrida. So he had taken the road back to Bordeaux, and shortly after that, in a fit of homesickness, left for Guadeloupe.

Back in Rivière au Sel, he had found Mira again, free, inaccessible, almost exactly as he remembered her. With their elbows resting on the bar at Chez Christian the men had lowered their voices to whisper to him the name of the person who was lying with her in sin and incest to give her what she wanted. But Carmélien had closed his ears to such silliness.

Suddenly, above the hammering of the rain on the corrugated iron roof, they heard the rumble of thunder. Turning his head towards the mountain, and slumped in the dark, Carmélien noticed a clearing in the sky and told himself that perhaps the fine weather would be back in the morning. For the time being the damp was making him shiver, and Carmélien looked around to warm himself up with some rum. Fortunately, Latifa, his mother's sister, was doing the rounds. He got closer, and from where he was sitting he could see the bottom half of the coffin. Cheap wood! But they weren't going to spend their money on a swine! The trunk had been empty, except for a few worthless papers, old letters and a pamphlet they had thrown in the bottom of a cupboard. Where had Moïse seen bundles and bundles of dollars? He must have been drunk that evening.

At first when Francis Sancher had turned up at Chez Chris-

tian, with Moïse clinging to him like a mosquito, Carmélien
hadn't found this tree of a man disagreeable. He had marveled at
Sancher's gift of gab, since he himself was shy and had difficulty
with words.

"Everything changed when my father died. My mother Térésa,
whose African blood had blackened her lips, drew me into the
study where he had spent his days and nights, like a spider
wrapped in the web of his business deals, and handed me the
papers that told the history of our family."

And then for someone who had only been to Bordeaux and
back with a spree to Barcelona that had misfired, all those names
he pronounced made Carmélien's head spin. Africa. America.
Cuba.

"Cuba?"

At that word, even those deadened by the late hour and the
rum, even the most inattentive, even the young people looking for
a role model, looking for hope to hang their impatience on,
crowded round the end of the bar, polished by generations of
drunkards, to drink in the words of Francis Sancher.

But he only shook his head.

"You won't like what I'm going to tell you about Cuba! You lot
only like stories round and juicy like California oranges. All you
want is sugar to sweeten your dreams. All I know are sad stories
to make you cry, sad stories to make you die! Everywhere I've
been, I've seen men and women tired of waiting for happiness,
their hands folded on their laps, tired of sowing without reaping,
tired of planting and being nipped in the bud. Do you want me to
tell you something? I'm glad the end is near."

"What end are you talking about?" the boldest would ask.

He would laugh. "Mine, of course! The only one that counts in
my eyes."

They laughed, even though there was one question on everybody's minds. Was he mad? Was he touched in the head like Dodose Pélagie's son, the unfortunate Sonny, who hangs about in the woods all day?

Yes, in the beginning, Francis Sancher hadn't seemed disagreeable to Carmélien. Then the affair with Mira broke like a clap of thunder. Deep down, people had smiled at the idea of rape. However hard Aristide shouted at the top of his voice, nobody believed him. He was given that sympathetic attention deserving of any man plunged in grief and who subsequently talks through his head. Everyone knew that the individual who could rape Mira Lameaulnes was not yet born. Not counting those who, in the secret of their hearts, said that Mira deserved a lesson from a man, ever since she had been leading them on in Rivière au Sel with her airs of "You won't get me to lie down for you!"

Carmélien, an inoffensive boy, had suddenly changed in character and dreamed of killing. Killing Francis Sancher. With a knife for killing the Christmas pig. Smearing over the ground the life of the person who had soiled his dream. When Mira had returned home with her belly and her shame to everyone's stupefaction, Carmélien's head had been filled with the craziest of ideas. He saw himself knocking at the Lameaulnes' door to ask for her hand. Now that she had fallen, Mira would have lost her arrogance and asked for nothing better than a young man to cover up her shame. He would crawl at her feet.

"Take me! Don't you know that a fallen woman must never give up hope? Don't you know you have seven lives to live? A life of perfect happiness begins with me! Guadeloupe has changed, you see. For better or for worse, I can't say. What I do know is that blacks, mulattoes and Indians, it's all the same. Take me!"

Nevertheless, the thought of Francis Sancher had stopped him dead in his tracks. What would he do if he met him coming down the road? If Sancher sniggered at him for eating his leftovers? For finishing a dish he had tired of? What would he reply? Would he be able to give him the good hiding he deserved?

Now Francis Sancher was dead. A secret hand had accomplished what his cowardice had never got round to doing. He would no longer have to bear his gaze or gouge his eyes out. The road was free.

Carmélien emptied his glass and felt like doing something incongruous, out of keeping, that would show the joy welling up inside him. He felt like bursting out laughing, letting out an oath or interrupting the drone of the women's prayers.

The rain didn't let up and the insects were gorging themselves with voluptuous cries of agony. He dreamed of taking off his clothes, as in the magical days of his childhood, and running naked under the refreshing raindrops.

Vilma

I wish I were my Indian grandmother who would have followed him to the funeral pyre. I would have thrown myself onto the flames licking over his body, and our ashes would have mingled as our souls never did. I wish I were my Indian grandmother who would have died for him. That's what I wish I were.

Our happiness did not have time to bud. Perhaps if he had lived beyond his allotted time, I would have managed to nurture that fragile plant which heat withers and rain devastates. Such as it is, our story is a sad one. He took me in;

you could say he kept me out of pity because I had come to seek refuge and he was not the type of man to leave a dog out in the rain.

Yes, I wish I were my Indian grandmother who would have followed him to the funeral pyre. Our ashes would have mingled and rained down on the Ganges.

If you want to know why I took refuge with him, a disreputable man, who one wretched morning loomed up in the middle of Rivière au Sel, you'll have to go back far, far into time to the day I was born, when the midwife shouted:

"A girl, Madame Ramsaran! The Good Lord has taken pity on you."

She never held my hand.

When she soaped me down as I stood naked under the sun, the palm of her hand was rough. When she took me to school, she walked three paces in front, and I'd stare at her black braid twisted into a chignon, held in place by a long tortoiseshell pin, while she presented me with her back under the black calico dresses that she wore every day the Good Lord made, in mourning for my sister Shireen. Shireen, dead at the age of three months, suffocated by the worms that had crawled up her insides to her mouth.

There was never any room for me in her heart. Nor for the boys either. Not even for Alix, the youngest, so handsome people called him "pitite a Bon Dié" (the Good Lord's child). But the boys had their papa who, as soon as school was out, took them across the fields, to soccer matches on Saturday and to the beach at Viard on Sunday where they hunted for gray clams in the gray sand.

I had nobody. I had nothing. Only my books.

"Where did she get all that intelligence from?" the school mistress marveled.

The other children refused to play with me. Out of jealousy they called me "Kouli malaba." Yes, all I had was my books. As soon as I got back from school I would lie down under my mosquito net and read and read until her rough voice found me where I had gone and brought me back to earth.

"Can't you hear when I'm calling you?"

That's why I can remember as if it were yesterday the day my father took me out of school, and I think I shall remember it until the day I die. For me it was the beginning of the end. It was a few weeks before school was due to start again. September had been fine, relatively dry for our region, smitten with the wind and the rain. The leaves glistened green under the golden rays of the sun. The fireflies danced in the dusk. The nights were humid with the dampness of our sweat. One of my cousins from the Grands-Fonds had spent the holidays with us and we'd been walking in the woods, going as far as the pond at Bois Sec, whose waters, it is said, turn to blood when the sun goes down and where the spirits come to drink.

That day we were finishing lunch.

She was fussing around Father, as she'd been doing for years and years, peeling a juicy, sticky brown sapodilla. Then she cut it into pieces and arranged them on a white saucer edged with blue. Without taking the trouble to thank her, Father stopped me as I was getting up from table.

"Let me tell you: you're not going back to school. It's a waste of time, I've got other plans for you!"

Nobody looked surprised, as if it were perfectly natural. I was speechless.

I ran out to my room, threw myself on my bed and started to

cry. Leaving school for me was tantamount to dying! After a while she came in and sat down on the bed.

"Listen," she said. "Your papa knows what he's doing. A woman is like an orange tree or a litchi. She's made to bear fruit. You'll see how happy you'll be when your belly swells out firmly in front of you and your child starts to kick in its haste to come out and warm itself in the sun."

Her eyes contradicted her words. You could sense she didn't believe a word, that she was reciting a lesson.

"I'm not interested in having children," I replied. "I don't want to get married."

She shrugged her shoulders and her mouth curled up in spiteful joy.

"But that's what's going to happen to you. I'm telling you so that you know, your father's made an arrangement with Marius Vindrex."

My tears dried instantaneously.

"What!"

Marius Vindrex is a sad-looking yellow man, as long as a rainy day, whose languishing eyes have not let me alone ever since I've been able to walk on my own two feet. He's got money, that's for sure! After having studied something or other in Canada, he started up his family's sawmill again. The logs arrive from Guyana, since our forests have been decimated, and all day long his machines whine, sawing wood, blackening the air with their smoke. He's Carmélien's good friend. Always talking politics with him. Last year, when a bomb killed that American, he was in seventh heaven; you'd think he'd placed it himself!

"Marius Vindrex?" I screamed. "But I don't love him!"

She sighed, then said in a tired voice:

"You watch too much *Dallas* and *Dynasty*. What does that

mean: 'I don't love him'? Do you think I loved your papa when I married him? And in India, in our country, don't you know that husband and wife didn't meet each other until they slept in the same bed, under the same sheets?"

I couldn't sit there listening to all her silliness. I went out. It was two o'clock in the afternoon. The sun was hammering down on my head. I felt madness running behind me, about to grab hold of me. I ended up on the Saint-Charles forest path, and at a turn I stumbled into the gully that was always cool and inviting with its dark, almost invisible waters, singing their little song under the ipecacs and the ferns:

> "Syé bwa
>   Légowine kasé
>   Syé bwa."[43]

A man was sitting on a rock watching the water. On hearing me, he stood up and stammered:

"Is it you? Is it you?"

Then his face closed up again.

"I'm sorry! I mistook you for someone else."

Considering how long I'd been hearing about the color and state of his clothes I had no trouble recognizing Francis Sancher and needed no introduction. I knew he'd just given a belly to Mira and that everyone was out for his blood. Personally, I don't like Mira Lameaulnes and I'm not afraid of her either. People believe her green eyes can turn them into dogs. People also believe that she can give hernias as big as banjos and erysipelas as heavy as yam seedlings. I just think her heart inside her breast is hard and gray as a rock. When she was at school, before they ended up expelling

---

[43] *Saw the wood/The handsaw is broken/Saw the wood.*

her, even though she was Loulou Lameaulnes's little darling, she used to arrive late after having roamed God knows where, sit down in her place, and while the other children recited their multiplication tables she'd hum the weirdest songs that nobody had ever heard before:

"*Chobet di paloud*
Sé an lan mè
An ké kontréw."[44]

What she had in her belly wasn't my problem.
"Who were you waiting for?" I asked Francis Sancher.
He stuck his bakoua hat on his hair that looked as though it hadn't seen a comb for months, and disappeared without even bothering to answer.

It was the wind. Blame it on the wind.
In the dark the mountain was sound asleep and the wind was lying at its feet. Suddenly, it shook itself and got up. It pressed up against the candlewood trees, then with one leap it rushed down to the savanna, overturning everything in its way. In its fury it blew into our house, throwing open doors and windows. She got out of bed to close them, and I heard Father order her to go and check the gate.
I felt anger and revolt boil up inside me. What's the point of a mother if she doesn't temper a father's egoism and cruelty? But for her, only Shireen counted. I could be sold like the last lot of hogplums in the market for all she cared! I had to make her ashamed, I had to hurt her, take my revenge. But how?

---

[44] *The whelk said to the clam,/I'll see you in the sea.*

Then, laughing like a madman, the wind whispered me the idea. Blame it on him! Blame it on the wind!

When I arrived at his house, the ferocious Dobermans, with their red muzzles, were fighting over a carcass. They left off to run towards me. But he made them lie down. He was sitting behind his typewriter.

"What do you want?" he asked, not in the least bit agreeable.

"Would you have a little job for me? Cooking or washing?"

He laughed. But even when he laughed, his eyes were as black as mourning.

"Here you are looking like an apsara,[45] and you want to work for me? It's the world upside down!"

I went closer.

"What are you doing?"

He laughed again.

"You see, I'm writing. Don't ask me what's the point of it. Besides, I'll never finish this book because before I've even written the first line and known what I'm going to put in the way of blood, laughter, tears, fears and hope, well, everything that makes a book a book and not a boring dissertation by a half-cracked individual, I've already found the title: 'Crossing the Mangrove.' "

I shrugged my shoulders.

"You don't cross a mangrove. You'd spike yourself on the roots of the mangrove trees. You'd be sucked down and suffocated by the brackish mud."

"Yes, that's it, that's precisely it."

He gave me the smaller of the two bedrooms. For a whole week I heard him scream and struggle with invisible spirits, call

---

[45] *An Indian nymph or temple maiden.*

for help and cry. I prayed the Good Lord would help him. Finally, at first light, he came to find sleep in my bed.

I didn't expect to love this man I had chosen in the great wind of madness. Love took me by perfidy. It crept stealthily into my heart and took possession of it . . .

But Francis Sancher was never mine. He was never Mira's either, that I know. The creature he belonged to was hiding in the shadows amid the sounds of the night.

The days were spent more or less peacefully. He wrote pages upon pages on the veranda. When he was tired of tearing them up, he went off into the woods, sometimes with the dogs, who returned with their tongues hanging out and their coats soaked. He didn't speak to me, he ignored me.

But as soon as darkness fell, everything changed. He drew close to me as if I could protect him.

Shaking, he would ask me:

"Can you hear him? Can you?"

I shrugged my shoulders and answered:

"Yes, I can hear the laughter of the wind that the night cannot keep under lock and key as it scours the countryside. Yes, I can hear the cavalcade of mangoes in a hurry to sink their stones into the belly of the earth so that they in turn can become eternal. I can hear the sea there in the distance endlessly quarreling with the rocks."

He found no consolation in these words. He went up to the window, peered into the night and said:

"Can you see him? Can you? He's standing there under the ebony tree. He's waiting for me. He's counting the days."

I went up to stare into the night over his shoulder and I could see nothing but high, dark, smooth walls.

"Come to bed," I begged him. "Doesn't my body taste nice?"

He wouldn't listen to me and went off to Chez Christian to

search for solace in rum. I stayed alone praying that one day he would find peace. When he returned he lectured me in a hollow and meaningless way. He told me about towns, he told me about all sorts of places, and I tried to find my way through his words without a guide.

"When we left Balombo it was dark. We had been fighting over this village for months. We had finally cleaned out the rebels. I had this smell of fresh blood in my nostrils that I couldn't get rid of. I had the death rattle in my ears of all those whom I let pass over to the other side without being able to provide comfort. There was this young girl, this child, I should say, with her legs torn off, who at the height of her suffering kept repeating: "Long live the Revolution!" But I was past believing in it. I couldn't take it any longer. It was that evening I put one foot in front of the other and became a deserter. The desert was white like salt under the moon."

I wanted to ask him questions. But he dozed off without even thinking of waiting for what I had to say. I watched him with his eyes closed and his mouth open, and I wondered through what wretched, arid lands this man's mind was roving. He never told me anything about himself, and I wouldn't know what truth there is in all those stories the people of Rivière au Sel tell.

When I was pregnant, I told him. He didn't say a word. Over our heads the rain continued to drum on the iron roof that the branches of the trees scraped every time the wind breathed. I touched his shoulder.

"Did you hear what I just said?"

He turned his back to me in answer and faced the wooden wall. From the shaking of his shoulders I realized he was crying. From that day on, he no longer took me in his arms, and we lived like father and daughter. When I was alone I made up sentences to soften his heart: "Why are you angry because my womb is fertile? For someone who is so afraid of death, don't you know that a child is the only cure?"

But when he returned, my words took fright at his impenetrable face, as hard as a rock, and flew away.

And now he's dead! All I have left is the memory, cold as ashes, of a little pleasure and a lot of pain. I confuse the past and the present.

I think I've never been closer to Francis Sancher than tonight, now that he has nothing left to say, now that he has gone and will never come back. Our ancestors used to say that death is nothing but a bridge between humans, a footbridge that brings them closer together on which they can meet halfway to whisper things they never dared talk about.

Amid the patter of the rain on the roof, the scraping of the trees, the rustling of the grass and the whistling of the wind as it steals between the badly joined planks of this house, I seem to hear his voice speak mysterious words I never heard before, lifting the enigma of who he was.

I wish I were my Indian grandmother who would have followed him to the funeral pyre. For then we would have gone on talking and talking.

Désinor, the Haitian

"I don't know why everyone is pretending to have a heavy heart. It would have made him laugh, that's for sure, after the way they treated him around here. But the people in Rivière au Sel are like that. They've got no feelings, and what's more, they're hypocrites. There's no use me lying. I didn't care a damn for Francis Sancher. I'm not going to take to mourning for the two hundred francs a week he gave me to fork over his garden! I'm here because I haven't smelled such delicious food or wet my throat with a good shot of rum for ages."

For the third time Désinor the Haitian went and filled his bowl with thick soup and looked with delight at the large marrow bone Madame Ramgoulam, Rosa Ramsaran's sister, was placing on a bed of cabbage, carrots and pumpkin. The hunger in his belly had been appeased, and he was helping himself again not only out of gourmandism but also in anticipation of tomorrow and the meager days to follow when there would be neither meat nor gravy. He ate voraciously, using his hands, and he could feel the look of contempt from his neighbors, who had skillfully served themselves with their spoons and placed a paper rectangle on their laps. He behaved so uncouthly on purpose and took delight in it. For once he was on an equal footing with the people of Rivière au Sel and wished he could have insulted them, shocked them and made them realize who in fact this Désinor Décimus really was, instead of taking him for a wretched Haitian gardener. It was only yesterday that Dodose Pélagie had given him one of her husband's old suits.

"Here, this is for you, Désinor."

He had almost thrown her jacket and trousers back at her face, so threadbare were they that you could see right through them, but he had gained control of himself and said what was expected of him:

"Thank you for your kindness!"

Earlier that week, he had just finished mowing her lawn, when Madame Théodose had called him in and pointed to some left-over sea-bream stew and a big slice of yam on a corner of the kitchen table. He had eaten because his belly wouldn't let him alone. Nevertheless, the bitter juices of his anger had got into the food.

That's why he had brought Xantippe along with him. To hurl a silent defiance at these petits-bourgeois. To shock them with their blackness. To shock them with their smell of poverty and destitution.

Désinor had arrived in Guadeloupe in November of 1980. November 2 to be exact, the day of the dead. This was no coincidence, as you can imagine, and his friend Baron Samedi[46] had leered at him from under his top hat, hinting that he was about to enter a realm of darkness and desolation. In fact, Désinor had dreamed of turning his back on his country for a long time. But in his mind, he had seen himself treading the sidewalks of New York that he already knew from Carlos's letters:

Brother Désinor,

I'm writing to let you know that I am in good health. You can find all the jobs you want in New York. Work is plentiful, all you have to do is bend down and pick it up. My room's big enough for two. I'm sending you the money for the journey . . .

Oh, that was so typical of Carlos! Two thousand miles apart and his heart still glowed with warmth. It was because they had grown up together, eaten out of the same bowl of poverty and sucked on the same dried-up breast of misfortune! They had mounted the same fleshy buttocks of the same Negresses, clinging to their coarse pubic hairs when they had been allowed to, which was seldom the case since they didn't have a cob[47] to their name. One day, tired of being refused by these heartless women, they climbed on each other, and to their surprise found the same flash

---

[46] *The Haitian spirit of the dead.*

[47] *Haitian money.*

of pleasure at the end of their lovemaking. So they had started all over again . . .

At first, Désinor had worked in the cane fields (still thriving for some people) over in Baie Mahault. Most of the cane cutters were Haitians like himself and exclamations were fired in all directions:

"Ou sé moun Jacmel tou?" (You're from Jacmel as well?)

Ah, the enslavement of the Haitian is not over yet! With great sweeps of his cutlass Désinor slashed his rage and his despair. At least back home there was always a bottle of rum to share, sweetening the taste of poverty.

One day, the news spread that the police were going to surround the field and ask everyone for his papers. Papers! Désinor had taken flight. The eternal flight of the black man from his misery and misfortune! He had run in a straight line, without even stopping to catch his breath, leaping over steep-sided gullies, climbing up hills and then suddenly, coming up against the forest, he had found himself in front of a sign reading "Rivière au Sel."

The place looked secluded and out of the way enough to discourage any overzealousness on the part of the police. You sensed that those living there were not in the habit of seeing farther than the end of their noses or breathing in anything but the smell of their breath. If the gendarmes came nosing around, they wouldn't get much out of these folk. So he had decided to lower his anchor at Rivière au Sel. He soon realized, however, that he had not been the only one to think along these lines. No less than a dozen men from Jacmel, Les Cayes and Les Gonaïves, recognizable by the very blackness of their skin and by the way they stole back furtively to their corrugated iron and mud huts, had settled together in a place called Beaugendre. And that's how they re-created their lost homeland as best they could.

Since Désinor had got it into his head to sit out his bad luck all on his own, he put as much distance as he could between Beaugendre and himself. This greatly upset the colony of exiled Haitians, who started to build fantastic stories about him. He was reported to be a "tonton-macoute" abandoned by kith and kin, one of Jean-Claude Duvalier's henchmen left behind after the dictator had fled to France to lead a life of luxury with the millions he had stolen, or a boko[48] hounded by angry loas.[49]

Désinor took no notice and went his own way. Ever since he had arrived in Rivière au Sel he had had the desire to be his own master, and made up his mind to offer his services as a handyman, digging up yams here, hoeing a patch of cassava there, fetching coconuts and pruning trees.

He propped a wattle hut up against a mango tree which, in season, dropped its fruit with the roll of a gwo-ka, and topped it off with two or three sheets of corrugated iron. Once he had made himself a stool and table out of a whisky crate, he felt a powerful feeling of ownership. In the dark he rested his weary bones on a kaban[50] and dreamed of New York, which now he realized he would never see. Or else he read over and over again the letters from Carlos:

> Brother Désinor,
> I'm writing to let you know that I'm in good health. I cannot believe what you told me. Guadeloupe is like any other country. You must be able to go somewhere else besides France. Make enquiries . . .

---

[48] *Sorcerer.*

[49] *Spirits.*

[50] *Bed.*

Désinor laughed. Carlos couldn't possibly understand. No, this place wasn't like any other place. The planes only went to Paris and back. People only traveled to French France!

Désinor lived two long years in this extreme solitude, his only company being the letters from Carlos that Moïse brought him regularly, often with a brotherly money order tucked inside. One morning, as he arrived at the crossroads, he saw a column of smoke curl up over the charcoal burners' hut. But it wasn't Justinien and his comely Josyna who had come back.

It was a man, as black as mourning and infinity, casting heavy looks of misfortune on people. His body was all skin and bone, vaguely covered in rags made from such a coarse cloth that it looked like jute. His feet were heavy and gnarled like Guinea yams. Despite his self-control, Désinor jumped and almost ran off as fast as his legs would carry him. Then he got hold of himself and murmured politely:

"Sa ou fè?"

The other mumbled an incomprehensible answer.

Three days later, while he was out fetching food for Dodose Pélagie's rabbits, once again he came across the character, standing like a dog on the prowl under a trumpet tree. With some difficulty he started up a conversation with him and learned that his name was Xantippe.

He discovered that Xantippe grew tobacco on his patch of land between his fruits and vegetables. A tobacco the likes of which Désinor hadn't tasted since he left the banks of the Artibonite. Once they were dried and rolled, the leaves gave you a smoke sweet enough to intoxicate the devil himself in Hell. The two companions made a habit of sitting opposite each other in the evening and communicating in silence amid the heavenly fragrance.

Désinor's heart was filled with the deep blue sky of Haiti or the powdery white of the sidewalks of Manhattan where Carlos sank up to his knees.

"I know I'll never see the Statue of Liberty," he grumbled. "Besides, they say she's nothing to look at and only looks kindly on those immigrants that are not like us. We're not the right color."

As for Xantippe, he was always grumbling about the same things. Something about a fire. Something about a hut burned to the ground. Something about a shower of sparks dancing in the midday sun. For a while, Désinor wondered whether Xantippe wasn't one of those arsonists who put the police on edge. He certainly looked like one! Besides, what was he doing roaming in the woods as soon as the cocks crowed? Until that day at Chez Christian when somebody recounted the unfortunate fellow's story with a great deal of assurance.

From that day on Désinor felt tied to Xantippe by a stronger bond. Who could be more miserable, more lonely than they were? Without wife, without children, without friends, without father or mother, with nothing under the sun.

For a moment the rain stopped hammering on the iron roof, and in the silence the choir of women could be heard:

"The Lord is in His holy temple,
The Lord, His throne is in Heaven;
His eyes behold, His eyelids try, the children of men."

Blessed was Francis Sancher on whom life had stopped sharpening its claws and who now had all eternity to rest! At that moment, Désinor's full stomach let out a loud belch and his neighbors looked at him, horrified by the presence of this vulgar nigger.

Dodose Pélagie

"I missed out on my youth, except for that episode blackened by the folly of sin. Old age is creeping on. In
the grimness of my heart I rejected and insulted this man
when he wanted to help me, and now I can do nothing to
make up for it."

At the age of fifteen when I walked through the streets of
La Pointe with my hair hanging down my back, the men
used to look at me and their eyes gleamed. At the lycée, I

came first in everything and the teachers said I would go far. Alas, that year my father, who worked for the Internal Revenue Services and every year took our small family to French France for the holidays, was carried off by typhoid. So my Mother Courage riveted herself to her piano stool and began to give lessons to the children of people she knew. Very quickly we realized that this wasn't enough, for with my two younger sisters and my little brother we were five. Five mouths to feed on scales, arpeggios and "le Clavecin bien tempéré."[51] I was wondering what I could do to help (enter the teachers' training college to become an elementary school teacher?) when one evening she called me into her room. On a low table an eternal flame burned in front of a picture of my father with his bushy mustache and his thick hair brushed back, away from the front.

"God is my witness," she sobbed. "It breaks my heart to say this, but Emmanuel Pélagie came to speak to me about you for the right reason. He would be a godsend in our desert!"

Emmanuel Pélagie! I knew Emmanuel Pélagie. I'd seen him at my father's funeral, straight as an I under the hot three-o'clock sun. Emmanuel Pélagie was the country's pride and joy. He was a very black man, not bad-looking, born in the Canal Vatable district to a poor woman. Despite that, he had become an engineer for the forestry commission and worked somewhere in Africa.

"I don't want to go to Africa," I stammered.

My mother took me by the hand.

"You won't have to. He doesn't want to go back. He wants to settle down here and find a wife."

"But why me?" I shouted. "Why me?"

My mother started to cry. Two months later I was married.

---

[51] A standard piano manual.

Perhaps another woman would have been beside herself with joy. My husband was the director of the research station for agronomy in Guadeloupe. We lived in a company villa in Le Gosier with seven acres of grounds. We entertained all sorts of people: the subprefect, French French on assignment, people from Martinique and Guyana, and once even a béké[52] with a "de" to his name. I ordered my dresses from the Trois Quartiers department store in Paris. Every evening there were fifteen to twenty places laid for dinner. From five in the morning my servants would be crumbling the crabmeat, making the flaky pastry and plucking fowl.

But I suffered martyrdom. I couldn't bear Emmanuel Pélagie. I couldn't bear the sound of his voice as he held forth at dinner:

"It's a mistake to believe that Africans and West Indians have anything in common, apart from the color of their skin. In certain cases, that is! Take my wife. You'd think she's Spanish! Our society is a society of cross-breeding. I reject the word 'Creole' that some are using. I've worked for five years on an okoumé plantation in the Ivory Coast. Precious wood, you know. And to speak to my employees I needed an interpreter. An interpreter! We couldn't communicate. As blacks we couldn't communicate!"

Or else:

"The law of March 19, 1946 has been drained of any meaning by every government since 1947, when the three-party system broke up. We need to form political parties demanding autonomy for Guadeloupe!"

I couldn't bear his laugh. I couldn't bear the smell of his mouthwash when he kissed me or his Jean-Marie Farina body cologne when he came near me. Fortunately he was so absorbed in

---

[52] *A white planter.*

himself that he didn't notice anything. Once he had taken his nightly pleasure, he would turn his back on me with the telling sigh of a state of well-being I couldn't share.

Apparently I was one of the few people who did not think highly of Emmanuel Pélagie. There was an unending stream of visitors through our living room. On days when he didn't work he held an audience. The telephone, which we were one of the first to have, never stopped ringing. It didn't take me long to find out what was behind it all. Emmanuel Pélagie was in politics. He had become a fervent admirer of a certain Rosan Girard and followed him about like a faithful dog. I heard him talk about war in Algeria, riots in Fort de France, and sporadic violence in Le Moule. It didn't interest me in the least. I shut my ears and I shut my heart.

Two or three years passed like that; Emmanuel Pélagie running to his political meetings, me busy doing the thousand-and-one nothings that make up the life of a middle-class housewife. My loathing for my husband grew by the minute. For he would say one thing and then do another.

Underneath all his fancy talk he secretly despised his fellow countrymen, and only felt at ease with the French French who streamed through our dining room. He would parade in front of them, playing *The Magic Flute* or *Madama Butterfly* on the record player. Never a béguine or a mazurka! During dinner I could never find anything to say to the French French sitting beside me, and wondered whether they were alive, if they had blood under their skin or were simply big white masks without sexuality or feeling.

Those were curious years for Guadeloupe! After dark, people would paint strange letters on walls that rang out like alarm bells. Offensive inscriptions such as "De Gaulle murderer" or "Down with colonialism!" I heard Emmanuel speak out about factories and unemployment of agricultural workers. He had meetings with doctors, lawyers and top civil servants like himself, who pretended to speak Creole among themselves and dared to address me with the words "Dodose sa kaye?" (How goes it, Dodose?)

It made me so angry to think that a few hours later Emmanuel would be tying his bow tie and singing *Madama Butterfly*.

One evening, during one of those endless dinners, I found myself sitting next to a young engineer from the Forestry Commission. He had blue eyes like the sky on a fine day. When the goat vol-au-vent was being served, he took my hand under the table.

Ah, Pierre-Henri de Vindreuil! My opinion about the French French changed overnight.

We used to meet in his high-rise apartment on the hill of Massabielle level with the rusty roofs of La Pointe. The hum of the town below mingled with our cries, then with our long intimate confidences following our embraces. For the first time I talked about myself and somebody listened. Oh, the infinite delight of it! I talked about my mother, who now had all she could wish for from Emmanuel. I talked about the sacrifice I had consented to at the age of sixteen. I talked about my sad marriage. On this last point, Pierre-Henri had trouble understanding me and expressed his surprise.

"He looks intelligent though!"

A woman doesn't need intelligence. How would you live with a genius? She needs tenderness, love!

Nothing came to warn me in my happiness that misfortune was slyly creeping up on me. I remember it was just before Christmas. Tall Christmas trees laden with artificial snow stood in the Lebanese shop windows, and when the offices closed there was a rush to order Yule logs from a fashionable cake shop behind the cathedral. The well-to-do went to French France, and I cursed the hypocrisy of Emmanuel Pélagie, who vetoed taking such a trip. How I too would have liked to dine on oysters and white wine in an elegant restaurant!

One afternoon Pierre-Henri suddenly announced he had been called back to Paris. I returned home, shattered, to find our veranda filled with men and women in tears. Emmanuel Pélagie had been beaten, then arrested by the police during a political meeting that had been banned by the Prefecture. He spent several days in jail. When he came out he was transferred for disciplinary reasons to the Research Station at Rivière au Sel to manage an experimental plantation of mahoganies from Honduras. His career was broken. Rivière au Sel!

I hate this dark, dank place. I look for the sky but it is hidden from the eye by the Spanish oaks, genipas and the giant mountain immortelles arching over the bay-rum and coral trees and the pink cedars, that in turn hang over the wild birchberry and guava trees. All these ageless creatures sink their heavy roots into the dark, spongy soil, while the creepers swing, pointing their forked tongues at face level, and the epiphytes feast voraciously on the trees and branches. While Emmanuel Pélagie watched over his mahogany saplings, I would walk as far as the pond at Bois Sec, among the tree ferns and the bamboo groves, praying to the Good Lord that one of the spirits, which this place is supposed to be infested with, would pounce on me and take away my meaningless life. After he left for French France on December 23, Pierre-Henri never wrote. As for Emmanuel, gone were the fancy speeches! Gone were the operatic arias! He withdrew into himself, as if he'd become deaf and dumb, and virtually stopped speaking to me. Sometimes I caught his look, as grave as the Last Judgment, and I shivered.

One morning, no sooner had I swallowed my first cup of coffee than I had a bout of nausea. I was pregnant. Pregnant! I took it the Good Lord was being bountiful. My baby gave me hope. While it kicked in the safety of my womb I told it:

"You shall be my refuge and my consolation. You shall be the youth I never had. You shall be my sunshine!"

Alas, I forgot the Good Lord breathes only vengeance!

A few hours after he was born, while I was basking in that postnatal peace and already imagining my life changed forever by this innocent little ball of flesh, Sonny, my newborn son, had a brain hemorrhage. Mentally handicapped for life!

When the doctors left us alone, face to face with our misfortune, Emmanuel Pélagie looked me straight in the eyes and said only: "It's your fault."

What did he mean? That's the question I've been asking myself ever since. Does Emmanuel Pélagie know it was the sin I committed over and over again with Pierre-Henri that was the cause of all this desolation in our lives? Just thinking about it, letting the memory of him work its way to the very depths of my soul, still sends a thrill through me. We have never sat down and talked about it, and day after day I have to live with this stony face opposite me.

You can easily understand that in my state of mind I had no time to waste thinking about Francis Sancher. I knew that Sonny was often at his house, but I couldn't stop him. The people of Rivière au Sel hate strangers. They hate them so much they'll say anything about them. When I first came here, I used to take the air of an evening with my unfortunate Sonny. All the shutters would be lowered as we went by, while invisible mouths whispered after us in slander:

"Look at them! She had her fling in La Pointe. And he's the cross the Good Lord sent her to bear."

"Now mind she hasn't come to do her dirty business around here."

So when Madame Mondésir told me that Francis Sancher was a makoumeh who did his perverted thing with Moïse, and Madame Poirier that he had been a gunrunner in Africa and hid his filthy lucre under his mattress, I didn't take any notice. Now it so happened that one evening I was coming back from a walk to Bois l'Etang when I met him. I like this place; it is supposed to be haunted by the spirits of our ancestors, who died and were buried during slavery. The sky is always gray and inked out by the knife-edge ridges of the mountain. Water lilies, duckweed and stiff tufts of grass carpet the dead eye of the pond, and the air is full of whispers, whistling noises and twittering. People avoid the place and I never meet anyone, except for that wretched Xantippe, whom I've seen several times cutting his way with a machete under the tall trees. I had gone back up by way of the Saint-Charles forest path, steep at this point under the shade of the pink cedars, when I came face to face with Francis Sancher.

I must confess that for a man no one could say anything good about, I was surprised by the gentle glow in his eyes, harking back to dreams that were still smoldering, to illusions still glimmering and to hopes churned by the rushing rivers of life. He walked straight up to me and greeted me very politely: "I was on my way over to your house, Madame."

I was immediately on my guard and asked:

"To my house? What were you thinking of doing at my house?"

He didn't let himself be taken aback by my rebuff, and went on to explain:

"I wanted to talk to you about Sonny. I'm a doctor, you know. This isn't my specialty, but—"

I interrupted him then and there.

"I don't need you to tell me how to look after my child."

And as he stood there staring at me without reproach, words

surged up into my mouth, coarse words, insults that rang out in the silence of the undergrowth, words that were not directed at him, but at life itself, which had been so unjust to me and buried my best years in this dismal jail. Then my words, my insults melted into water, bitter with all my grief.

That's the way it happened. This man, who loved my poor child who is so much in need of love, is dead. My pain and my regret at not having listened to him still haunt me. And yet he showed me the way.

I started to ask myself questions in the secret of my heart. Do I really love my unfortunate Sonny? Isn't he just a cross that I long to lay down? Isn't he a constantly open wound to my pride? A painful incarnation of my remorse? Or a punishment inflicted on Emmanuel, whom I continue to hate but have never known how to leave? I must put an end to all this. From now on, I'll take care of Sonny. I'll knock on the door of every hospital, every clinic and dispensary. I'll lay siege to every doctor. I'll try every new treatment. I'll go to the end of the world, if need be. I'll leave Emmanuel, locked in his bitterness, and Rivière au Sel stuck in its perpetual meanness.

Yes, there is a time to seek and a time to lose; a time to keep and a time to cast away; a time to rend and a time to sew; a time to keep silent, and a time to speak; a time to love, and a time to hate.

Now is the time for me to start over again.

Lucien Evariste

"When I think how mistaken I was about him! I took him to be a barbudo[53] from the Sierra Maestra, a builder of worlds, whereas in fact he belonged to that highly dangerous species who has lost all illusions and demolishes what he once adored. Yet I loved him like a friend."

Lucien Evariste had remained a long time with the men under the tarpaulin during this night that was the color of

---

[53] *A companion of Fidel Castro in the Sierra Maestra.*

rain. He now stepped into the room where the dead man lay, not to pray, but to warm himself from the heat of the candles and litanies. Lucien hadn't recited a Hail Mary for years, even less a Confiteor Deo, even though he had been a choirboy, and his mother had dreamed of giving a priest to the church as she looked at him lovingly in his surplice. She had given birth to her boy late in life, and wondered what she had done to the Good Lord, tired as she was of accumulating over fourteen years of sperm for nothing from her fiery husband, the Dr. Evariste, who had his surgery next door to the presbytery and the cathedral, but who at night paid scant attention to God's commandment: thou shalt not be lustful. A latecomer, Lucien had grown up wrapped in lace and linen. He had been fed on fine wheaten flour and soothed on orange blossom. At the age of seven, sitting in pew no. 32 in the cathedral between his mother and father, he would turn the pages of a big missal and sing the hymns in tune:

"O God, our conqueror,
Save our France,
In the name of the Sacred Heart."

You can imagine how his parents suffered when he became a revolutionary and an atheist!

It had all begun quite by chance. While he was quietly studying for a classics degree in Paris he had gone along with a friend to a demonstration out of pure curiosity. He hadn't gone a hundred yards along the rue des Ecoles when a ruffian from the police riot squad tore off half his ear with a billy club. This unjust mutilation had determined his future, and from that day on he had become one of the pillars of student protest, whatever the cause. Back home, his mother was upset. But his father shrugged his shoulders and told her over and over again she was wrong to get into such a state. Once their son was back in the warm Caribbean sun, he'd soon forget all about those ideas. Hadn't those who'd refused to fight in Algeria now returned to the fold and drew their salaries from the state budget? But for once, his father's knowledge, infallible in cases of duodenal ulcers or inflammation of the pleura, proved him wrong. When he returned, Lucien refused to live under the family roof, and after making a great fuss about joining the patriotic cause he became an editor at Radyo Kon Lambi in charge of the program *Moun an tan lontan* (People of Yesteryear), in which he told the stories of the heros, martyrs, patriots, leaders and major figures who had died naturally, or more often violently, in their struggle to get the wretched of the earth to rise up and march. For every word he uttered, his mother—glued to the radio —asked for the Good Lord's forgiveness. For her, to talk about the class struggle or the exploitation of man by man was as bad as talking about fornication or adultery. To symbolize his break with his family, who believed that you marry people of the same color and the same-size bank account, Lucien moved in with Margarita, a black-skinned girl he met at a market stall in Petit-Canal. Margarita couldn't put three words of French together, but was now desperately trying, much to the amusement of their neighbors.

Lucien was glad to be back home as soon as he had finished his MA. More often than not, though, he poignantly bemoaned the torpor of this sterile land that never managed to produce a revolution. If only he'd been born somewhere else! In Chile! In Argentina! Or just a stone's throw away, in Cuba! Triumph or die for freedom!

In order to occupy the evenings that Margarita spent thrilling to the television adventures of American heiresses, Lucien got it into his head to write a novel. But he could get nowhere, wondering whether to write a historical portrait tracing the heyday of the Maroons or a romanticized saga of the great slave revolt of 1837 in the South. His patriot friends, whom he widely consulted, were just as hesitant, some in favor of the Maroons, others in favor of the revolt in the South, but all bidding him to write in his mother tongue, Creole. Lucien, who at the age of six had been slapped by both parents for having said out loud the only Creole expression he knew: "A pa jé?" (Are you joking?) was in a dilemma and, without daring to admit the fact, looked helplessly at the expensive electronic typewriter he had just bought. It was Carmélien Ramsaran who told him about Francis Sancher living in Rivière au Sel.

Carmélien and Lucien had become friends from grilling themselves in the Saturday afternoon sun at the soccer stadium and cursing the local team's goalkeeper. They often got together and annoyed Margarita with the noise of their squabbling, for Carmélien took after his father, Sylvestre, who boasted he had never voted in his life. Whenever Lucien started off on one of his ideological speeches, Carmélien would bring him back to earth in a mocking tone of voice: "Open your eyes, man. We're already European. Independence is a sleeping beauty that no prince will ever wake up."

A Cuban in Rivière au Sel! A Cuban! Lucien, who knew all about Fidel Castro's adventures in the Sierra Maestra, who had taken his side in his quarrel with Che Guevara, who had watched admiringly *La Ultima Cena* dozens of times during Third World Film Festivals and who knew the number of Soviets in Cuba down to the last man, had never seen a Cuban with his own two eyes. Except perhaps the musicians of the Sonora Mantecera orchestra who were all the rage in the Latin Quarter when he was a student. But they were Cubans living in Miami, exiles, counterrevolutionaries!

A Cuban in Rivière au Sel! What was he doing there?

Carmélien made a face.

"He says he's a writer."

"A writer?"

Lucien jumped, thinking of Alejo Carpentier and José Lezama Lima, and already saw himself discussing style, narrative technique, and the use of oral tradition in writing. Usually, such a discussion was impossible, since the few Guadeloupean writers who did exist spent most of their time holding forth on Caribbean culture in Los Angeles or Berkeley. However hard Carmélien tried to dampen his enthusiasm, adding that in his opinion Sancher was one of those undesirables Castro had thrown out of the country because of their vices, Lucien wouldn't listen. A Cuban in Rivière au Sel! How could he get to meet him?

After thinking it over, Lucien decided to send him a detailed epistle inviting him to one of the programs on Radyo Kon Lambi. Many weeks went by without an answer. He would watch for the postman's yellow van, walk as far as the post office and tell everyone in hearing he was expecting an important letter—all in vain. Against the advice of Margarita who, for her part, had heard nothing good about Francis Sancher, Lucien made up his mind to pay him a visit, a common practice to welcome newcomers in the villages and hamlets. Thank goodness they were not in La Pointe where the slightest visit had to be preceded by a telephone call.

Lucien made feverish preparations for this meeting. He had a copy made of his best programs, in particular the one broadcast the day after Cheikh Anta Diop[54] died, with an elementary school teacher from Benin, who miraculously was teaching at Anse Bertrand. He spent nights drafting outlines of his two novels, only to tear up in the morning what he had gone to great lengths to devise during the hours of darkness. Finally, fearing that he would look pretentious, he decided to go empty-handed.

---

[54] *A Senegalese philosopher who revolutionized contemporary thinking by claiming that Ancient Egypt was a black civilization.*

He arrived in Rivière au Sel one evening on the stroke of six, with his heart thumping as if he were about to take a test.

Despite his beard, Francis Sancher looked nothing like a barbudo.

With his shirt wide open, showing the curly hairs of his chest, Sancher was staring at his typewriter as if it were a rival with a familiar temper. He looked up at Lucien with magnificent misty eyes floating with dreams and derangement and exclaimed:

"A letter? What a strange idea! I only open my bills. And what did it say?"

Paralyzed by emotion, Lucien floundered with the short speech he had prepared in the bus. Francis Sancher listened with a fatherly grin on his lips, went and fetched a bottle of rum and two glasses, then said:

"You've knocked on the wrong door, my son. May I call you that? The person you see standing in front of you can only tell of men and women whose lust for life has been cut short. Just like that! No glorious struggle. I've never heard the names of those you mention. I'm not what you think I am. I'm more or less a zombie trying to capture with words the life that I'm about to lose. For me, writing is the opposite of living. I confess to impotence."

Lucien cried out in indignation, ascertaining that literature was the necessary extension of a struggle, calling Césaire and his miraculous weapons to his rescue. Francis Sancher burst out laughing.

"I used to speak like that."

"When?"

He poured himself a glass of rum big enough to make a good-size fighting cock lose its head, and then continued:

"And first of all I'm not a Cuban. I was born in Colombia, in Medellín. When she was seven months pregnant my mother left the plantation, as was the custom, and went and waited for my

birth at her parents', two old bourgeois fossilized in their prejudice, living in one of the few lovely old houses of that horrible
industrial city, next door to the church of San José. She almost
died giving birth, and while they were fighting for her life, they
left me in a corner covered in blood and fecal matter where the
midwife forgot about me for forty-eight hours. I should have died
there and then!"

"But you did go to Cuba?"

"Cuba? Later, much later!"

"Did you fight? Did you fight?"

In the middle of that question Moïse the Mosquito arrived and
was greeted by the furious barking of the dogs who, strangely
enough, had hardly wagged their tails at Lucien. Lucien was not
the type to listen to gossip, but he thought the newcomer had a
sour face, like the one Margarita put on when he talked for hours
with an intruder. Francis Sancher ignored Moïse and continued on
his tangent:

"My father had a large wine-colored mark on his face that
washed around his cold little shark-like eyes. I always think of
him as being dressed in black, probably because his whole being
reminded me so much of death. In fact, he most likely wore heavy
white cotton suits, starched stiff by our numerous servants. Every
evening my mother made my brother and myself kneel down at
the foot of his bed in his big, red-tiled bedroom and pray for him
with our eyes staring at the crucifix. We knew a curse was hanging
over the family."

At this point Moïse stared at Lucien as if to say:

"Completely nuts! Don't you think he's completely nuts?"

While Lucien, who had more or less recovered his wits, jibed:

"A curse? You're talking like a field nigger!"

"A curse, I'm telling you! That takes the form of a sudden,
unexplained death, always around the same age, in the early fifties.

My grandfather was struck down on horseback while he was coming back from a card game where he had been cheating as usual. My great-grandfather died the morning after a night when he hadn't even made love to his favorite mistress, Luciana. My great-great-great-grandfather drowned the morning after his second wedding in the swamps of Louisiana, where he had taken refuge after fleeing from Guadeloupe . . ."

Lucien jumped.

"What's that you're saying? Guadeloupe?"

"Oh, I haven't told you anything yet. Papers prove that it all starts from here."

"Here?"

"Have you heard of the Saint-Calvaire Great House?"

"Saint-Calvaire? I'm not a historian. Ask Emile Etienne."

Their first meeting ended with everyone rolling drunk, and Lucien almost plunged into the river Moustique on his way back to Petit-Bourg.

Two days later he came across Emile Etienne down on the rue Frebault in La Pointe, and asked him about it. But Emile Etienne shrugged his shoulders and called Francis Sancher's remarks "bullshit" with no historical basis.

Eaten away by curiosity, Lucien had gone back to see Francis Sancher to try and piece together the puzzle of his life.

"So you were a military doctor?"

"You could call it that. You know when they started to be wary of me? When I started taking pity on the Portuguese. I too used to think they were a bunch of bastards who had bled the country white and deserved what they got. And then in a room next to mine at the Hotel Tivoli, Doña Maria was dying of cancer. Using the excuse that she was doomed to die, her husband had grabbed all her jewels, necklaces and aigrettes and taken the first plane to Lisbon. During the very rare moments when she wasn't suffering torture I stole up to her bedside and read to her from her favorite novel, *The Brothers Karamazov:* 'A man must remain hidden in order to be loved.' "

What should he make of all these cock-and-bull stories? Lucien asked himself. What should he make out of them?

He couldn't solve the enigma. But through drinking glass upon glass of straight rum with Francis Sancher, his liver gave him hell, and Margarita cursed him when she received the full blast of his breath.

Soon information began circulating from another source, from Sylvanie, Emile Etienne's wife, who reported or distorted her husband's words. Going by what she said, Francis Sancher thought himself the descendant of a white Creole planter, cursed by his slaves, who had come back to haunt the scenes of his past crimes. Although the intellectuals were skeptical about such stories, common folk reveled in them, and everyone spied on Francis Sancher when he came down to the village to replenish his supply of rum, finding that in fact he did have the look of a cursed man. The women secretly had a soft spot for this mastic-bully of a man, so tall and straight under his silvery head of hair. But the men couldn't stomach him and called him all sorts of names.

"It's true, man. It's true. Before he was washed up here, body and soul, he dumped his load of dirty business in the world, like his father before him!"

At night when Margarita told this gossip to Lucien as they lay in bed together, he got angry.

"How can you repeat such nonsense?"

For as time went by, and weeks turned into months, Lucien forgot the original ideological reasons for his interest in Francis Sancher and quite simply grew fond of him. He was the big brother and young father he never had, joking and tender, a cynic and a dreamer. During the so-called rape episode with Mira and the seduction of Vilma there was no more ardent defender of Francis Sancher than Lucien.

"In this country, a man's sexual life is a swamp which it is better to steer clear of. Why do you want to drain this one?"

And he would remind all and sundry of the girls they had got pregnant, the virgins they had had and the papaless children they had sowed to the wind.

The friendship between Lucien and Francis Sancher was not to everyone's liking. The Patriots living in the area found a way of taking offense and complaining. Instead of preaching an example here was the editorial writer of Radyo Kon Lambi making friends with a suspicious character. For by adding two and two together you could get a certain idea of Francis Sancher's dubious life. Consequently, Lucien was summoned in front of a genuine tribunal and asked to explain himself, which he did.

"Listen, gentlemen! For a long time I thought like yourselves that you had to eat patriotically, drink patriotically and screw patriotically. I divided the world in two: us and the bastards. Now I realize it's a mistake. A mistake. There's more humanity and riches in that man than in all our lecturers in Creole."

Following that, the program *People of Yesteryear* was taken off the air, but Lucien didn't give two hoots, since he spent almost every evening hanging on Francis Sancher's every word.

"The ground was dry and white under the moon. We knew that death could come from any direction, and we waited for it, philosophically. I closed my eyes and made a film go through my head. I saw the face of a woman I'd met one Carnestolado Fiesta day in Sinaloa."

"A woman? I thought you didn't like women?"

"I said I'm leery of them, it's not the same. I've screwed more women than you'll ever screw, even if you live to a hundred and seven. My finest memory, you know, was the time when we recaptured a village. Exhausted, I entered a compound thinking it was deserted. A girl, almost a child, her breasts hardly showing, was huddled up on a mat. On seeing me she uttered a cry of fright. I can still smell her virgin blood in my nostrils."

"Where was this?" Lucien asked in a very Cartesian fashion. "When you were in Angola?"

But Francis Sancher was already far away and not answering.

The flames of the candles melting slowly into the saucers cast animal shadows on the wall. Lucien couldn't believe his friend— silent for once—was there in this roughly-hewn, cramped wooden box, and a stream of salt water surged up to his eyelids. He went up to the coffin as if Francis Sancher was about to tell him through the glass that the joke was over and he was coming back to take his place in the world and reveal what he had hidden for such a long time.

It's true, death is amazing! One day, a man is here. Talking, laughing, looking at women with passion uncurling in his crotch. The next, he's as stiff as a board.

What tribute could he pay to his friend who had disappeared so suddenly?

Then an idea germinated in Lucien's bruised mind. Shy and hesitating at first, as if preposterous, it soon came into its own and wouldn't leave him alone. Instead of hunting down Maroons or nineteenth-century peasants, why not, as an urban son of the twentieth century, put together Sancher's memories end to end, as well as snatches of his personal secrets, brush aside the lies and reconstitute the life and personality of the deceased? Oh, this idealist without an ideal was not going to make it easy for him. He would have to reject the power of generally accepted ideas. He would have to look dangerous truths in the face. He would have to displease. He would have to shock.

And to write this book, wouldn't he have to track down his hero? Check out the footprints he had left along the paths of life? Put himself in Sancher's shoes?

Europe. America. Africa. Francis Sancher had traveled all these lands. So shouldn't he do the same? Yes, he too would leave this narrow island to drink in the smell of other men and other lands. It seemed to him that this was the opportunity he had secretly been dreaming of since his return home, since he had buried all his energy and led a hopeless struggle. With renewed enthusiasm he felt in a conquering mood, ready to leave on a great adventure, and he cast a triumphant look around him.

He saw his book published by a leading publisher on the Left Bank in Paris, acclaimed by the press, but coming up against local critics.

"Is this novel really Guadeloupean, Lucien Evariste?"

"It's written in French. What kind of French? Did you ever think of writing in Creole, your mother tongue?"

"Have you deconstructed the French-French language like the gifted Martinican writer Patrick Chamoiseau?"

Oh, he'd know how to defend himself and answer them back!

A healthy impatience burned through his veins. He looked feverishly across the room where the women had ended up dozing off, their rosaries hanging loosely from their fingers, their lips huskily mouthing:

> *"We give thanks unto Thee, O God;*
> *We give thanks for Thy name is near:*
> *Men tell of Thy wondrous works."*

It was then that Emile Etienne the Historian, who had discreetly stayed outside with the men, entered the room, the glow from the candles reflecting off his receding forehead. He took hold of the small branch, dipped it in the holy water, and clumsily sprinkled the coffin. Impatient as he was, Lucien almost walked over to him and demanded he tell everything he knew about Francis Sancher. Was it true what people were saying? Had he been his confidant? Lucien gained control of himself in time, casting Emile Etienne a threatening look that puzzled Emile, since they had often worked together on *People of Yesteryear* and were generally on excellent terms.

Mira

Even though I have resigned myself to not knowing who he was, Quentin, my son, will not be inclined to do
the same. He'll set off like Ti-Jean and travel the world on
horseback, stamping the ground with his hooves of hatred,
stopping at every cabin, every hovel and every Great House
to ask:

"Ou té konnet papa mwen?" (Did you know my father?)

He'll hear and get all sorts of answers. Some will say:

"Oh my, he was a vagabond who came to bury his rotten

self here. We don't even know whether he was white, black or Indian. He had every blood in his body."

Others will say:

"He was crazy and talked out the top of his head, out the top of his head!"

And yet others will say:

"He was a malefic man who bewitched two of our loveliest maidens. A ragamuffin, I'm telling you!"

But I have to know the truth.

I'll never go down to the gully again. It too betrayed me. Like Rosalie Sorane, my mother, who abandoned me to solitude from the first day I came into this world. The fruit it gave me to calm the hunger of my heart was, in fact, poisoned.

I, Mira, the wild thing with no collar or leash, I didn't realize there was pleasure in serving, giving, even humiliating myself.

He would laugh at me.

"Woman, as in all good families, you were taught that the best way to keep a man is through his stomach. I'm telling you that nothing will keep me. Neither head, nor heart, nor stomach, nor sex. Nothing. I'm just passing through. Before you came, you know, I had never screwed a woman more than once, scared she would keep me prisoner of her thighs."

As he stood on the veranda, his eyes roved the horizon.

"I wish that little volcano you keep your eye on every morning, that scares you so much, I wish it would recover its former strength and explode. EXPLODE. A sun, brighter than the sun itself, would flash out of its crater mouth. Sulfur ash would be spewed out as well and we would all die. All buried without having the time to catch our breath. To die alone, one time and one time only, that's what's so terrible!"

"Why do you always talk about dying?" I protested. "You're as firm on your feet as a mapou tree."

I couldn't get him to smile and he shook his head.

"Me a mapou? If I told you the truth, you'd run a mile."

"Tell me the truth."

But he didn't say another word. And to this day I don't know anything. So I have to discover the truth. From now on my life will be nothing but a quest. I shall retrace my steps along the paths of this world.

I can guess what they are all thinking. My father thinks that after the Good Lord has been so bountiful in dealing out misfortune, I'll keep my eyes lowered in his presence and spend my days repenting. I'll become a zombie at mealtimes, putting my hand over my child's mouth to stifle his voice. Aristide imagines I'll find my way back to his bed as if nothing has happened. Dinah thinks I shall join the growing flock of those that bleat and graze far from their shepherd. Nothing of the sort will happen. They're all mistaken.

My real life begins with his death.

Emile Etienne, the Historian

"It's almost as if men keep a streak of insanity in the hollow of their heads. Neither learning nor education can come to terms with it. Here's a man who had nothing to fear about anything and who's dead because he was scared to death."

Having thus philosophized, Emile Etienne realized he had a good way to go, back to Petit-Bourg, and walked up to the coffin. He had a heavy heart, since he had been very attached to Francis Sancher. The funeral would be a tiresome formality during which everybody would be sweating in his Sunday best under the three-o'clock sun with one idea in mind: let's get it over with and go home. The time had come to bid farewell.

Emile Etienne sprinkled the coffin with holy water, thinking this was the first time he had seen his friend silent and lifeless, he who usually thrived on the sound of words. That's how he had first made Sancher's acquaintance at Chez Christian, when Emile had seen him propping up the counter, drinking his rum like a regular, and declaring:

"Friendship of the Prince! I shall return each season with a chattering green bird on my fist!"

People were nudging each other, while Emile looked on in surprise, for he thought he knew everyone in Rivière au Sel by name, father and grandfather.

"Where did he spring from?"

"He's the one who bought the Alexis property," Tall Fernand guffawed.

Emile Etienne had become interested in the Alexis property when people had started to recount the strange goings-on there, and how it must be haunted by the spirits of the ancestors. Yet when he consulted his notes, they gave little credibility to the theory. Its genealogy, in fact, was of little interest. A magistrate from La Pointe, a French Frenchman by the name of Perier du Marcilhac, had bought twenty to thirty thousand square feet of land around 1920 and built a small "change of air" house on it.

Rivière au Sel's reputation was no better today than it was years ago. Situated in the midst of the dense rain forest, it was a wet spot. The dismal sand of the nearest beach at Viard had no attraction for bathers, who headed for the sun and golden shores of Grande Terre. Was that why Perier du Marcilhac hadn't hung around for very long? Two years later he sold his estate to Juste

Alexis, an elementary school teacher in Petit-Bourg. At that time, elementary school teachers took pride of place, and Juste ensconced himself with his wife in his pew at church, clicking his heels triumphantly as he followed her to the altar. That's what Emile Etienne had told Francis Sancher when the latter approached him on hearing he was called the Historian.

Francis Sancher had seemed disappointed.

"Is there a Great House called Saint-Calvaire in the neighborhood?" he persisted.

Emile Etienne thought the matter over.

"Saint-Calvaire? Not that I know of. But I'll check. Are you a historian, my friend?"

Francis Sancher laughed bitterly.

"Me? History's my nightmare."

It was quite by coincidence that Emile Etienne had been bitten by the history bug, since he was a nurse by profession. Every day he drove up to Dillon to stick a syringe into the buttocks of Fleurival Fleuret, an eighty-year-old, who day after day bored him to death with his chatter, until suddenly, for some unknown reason, Emile had pricked up his ears.

"You mean to say you went to Madagascar?"

"Like I said! I used to work in the hostel for Madagascan students on the rue de Rennes in Paris, and one of the residents, who was returning to Madagascar, invited me to go with him. And off I went. A few years after my arrival, war broke out. White soldiers, Senegalese infantrymen . . ."

Dumbfounded, Emile Etienne drank in every word. He recalled his dismal history lessons, and the boring list of battles lost and won. Why not approach things from a different angle, collecting testimonies that relived the actual events?

This was how *Let's Talk About Petit-Bourg* came into being, representing two years of hard work, once the day's injections and massages were over with. Two years of wooing the old folks, tracking down their reluctant thoughts. He'd also given Deschamps the printer all his savings.

Alas, predictably, the intellectuals of La Pointe had poked fun at his work, pointing out printing errors and mistakes in style, and Emile Etienne had only sold about fifty copies to his most steadfast patients; the remainder were still yellowing on the shelves of the bookstore La Librairie Générale. Deeply hurt, Emile Etienne dreamed of revenge as he wound and unwound his bandages.

When Christian had put everyone out, Francis Sancher invited Emile Etienne to stay up the rest of the night with him, adding, mysteriously, that he wanted to show him certain documents.

Singing a popular drinking song of that time, they had walked down the road arm in arm. On reaching the house, Francis Sancher placed a bottle of rum between them and pulled out of a trunk some old papers, letters and title deeds dating back to 1790 for a sugar plantation of a thousand acres situated at Saint-Calvaire, Petit-Bourg, issued to a certain François-Régis des Sallins, as well as a slim, anonymous pamphlet published by John Russell Smith in London in 1862 entitled "Wonders of the Invisible World."

Leafing through the latter, Francis Sancher had whispered:

"You have here the entire history of my family, written by a descendant who believed he could escape the punishment by fleeing across the English Channel. Alas, he too died at the age of fifty from a mysterious nose bleed."

Not knowing any English, Emile Etienne had asked Francis Sancher to translate for him. Then Emile shrugged his shoulders.

"Let's be serious. You're not telling me you believe in all this nonsense? These are pearls of popular folklore that make it a unique and precious form of expression."

From that time on, whenever they met, the two men avoided

such subjects. Occasionally, Emile Etienne would poke fun at Francis Sancher, nicknaming him "The Cursed One," or tease him when he saw him prick up his ears, stare into space or kick up a fuss for no reason:

"Now tell us what you can see!"

Noticing the effect the wretched Xantippe had on Francis Sancher, Emile Etienne referred to him as "The Go-Between" and laughingly asserted that Xantippe did look as though he came from another planet. When they were together, Emile Etienne spoke mainly about himself, and his one ambition:

"I'd like to write a history of this island that would be based solely on the memories kept in the hollow of our minds and the hollow of our hearts. What fathers told their sons and mothers told their daughters. I'd like to travel north and south, east and west, collecting all those words that have never been listened to . . ."

Francis Sancher approved.

"What's stopping you?"

Yes, what in fact was stopping him?

Looking at the coffin, Emile Etienne suddenly felt ashamed of his cowardice. What was he frightened of? Being scoffed at by the pedants? He felt filled with an immense courage and renewed energy that flowed mysteriously through his veins.

Yes, he would set to work the very next day. This was the promise he made to his friend that would keep them united beyond the grave. He knelt down. After a while, his eyes brimming with tears, he stood up and went out onto the veranda. Amid guffaws of laughter, Jernival the cabinetmaker was telling how after drinking a concoction of hardwood he got a hard-on! Wow, what a hard-on!

Emile Etienne cast a look of reproach at all these laughing faces and was surprised to see Xantippe's, stony and inscrutable, among them. The wretch always stood apart from everything and everyone, wandering silent and mute like a zombie, looming up where you least expected him. Emile Etienne, who had grown up among his father's tomatoes and okras, noticed that Xantippe had planted an authentic Creole garden on the patch of land he squatted, using the old ways now long forgotten. Emile Etienne had consequently tried to approach him with a tape recorder, but all he had got were some undecipherable mumblings.

Emile Etienne nodded to the offended fathers, Loulou Lameaulnes and Sylvestre Ramsaran, then looked beyond the perimeter lit by the electric lightbulbs. The weather was not letting up. The wind and the rain continued their dismal pranks, and the moon was hiding behind a low wall of dark clouds. He would have to drive carefully. Two days earlier, a coach filled with tourists had plunged into the river Moustique and made front-page news in *France-Antilles*.

With these new ideas haunting him, this was not the time to die. What would he call this monumental work that would give meaning to his life? Words buzzed in his head. This time he would put up a fight and make a name for himself. And once he had shown these so-called intellectuals what he could do, he would turn his back on them and leave. At last!

Emile Etienne remembered his joyless childhood as a little black-skinned boy, out of the womb of a poor woman, sitting at the back of the class from first grade to sixth grade. His teens had been morose. At the local dances the girls would hide from him, nicknaming him "Black Treacle." Through a series of scholarships and sacrifices by his mother, Estella, he had, nevertheless, managed to pass his baccalauréat. But then Estella had come to the end of her resources, and he in turn had been forced to help his sister Bergette and his brother Rosalien. He had had to be content with watching the planes leave from the visitors' terrace at Le Raizet airport, and make do with his studies as a nurse. Ever since, he had been crisscrossing the region of Petit-Bourg, as familiar a figure at the wheel of his Peugeot as Moïse in his yellow van.

Leave. Breathe a less rarefied air. He suddenly seemed to be suffocating under the tall trees, and he dreamed of a land where the eye would not be blackened by the hills but could follow the unlimited curve of the horizon. A land where, despite what they say here, the color of one's skin doesn't matter.

A homeland where the soil would be rich for plowing.

Xantippe

I named all the trees of this island.

I climbed to the top of the hill and cried their name, and they answered my call.

Candlewood. Mastwood. Bladdernut. Golden spoon. Trumpet wood. Myrtle. Incense tree. Magnolia. Cigarbox cedar. Crabwood. Resolu. Star apple. Saltfish wood. Sweet plum. Manjack. Marmalade tree. Mapou.

The trees are our only friends. They have taken care of our bodies and souls since we lived in Africa. Their fragrance is magic, a power recaptured from times long gone by. When I was little, Maman used to set me down under the shade of their leaves, and the sun would play hide-and-seek above my face. When I became a Maroon, their trunks barricaded me in.

I too named the vines. Bird's-nest anthurium. Oilcloth flower. Little star jasmine. Goosefoot. Morning glory. Firecracker. The vines too are our friends from long, long ago. They tie body to soul. They lock creeper on creeper.

I named the gullies, gaping vaginas at the bottom of the earth. I named the rocks at the bottom of the water, and the fish, as gray as the rocks. In a word, I named this land. It spurted from my loins in a jet of sperm.

For a long time I lived in the hollow of the wild pineapples, filling my belly with the sap from the trees. Sometimes I was tired of roosting in the treetops and flew down to the savannas among the sugarcane in flower. I turned my back on the hills and headed for the sea, seeking the muddy lowlands eaten away by the brackish water of the marine culs-de-sac. I loved the black sand, black as my skin and the mourning in my heart.

Long ago I lived with Gracieuse. Gracieuse. My ebony-black woman. My juicy Kongo cane. My embroidered malavois,[55] melting under the palate of my mouth.

One day I was washing my old clothes in the river when she appeared in front of me, her tray balanced on her head.

"Is that a man's work you're doing there?" She laughed huskily.

"No, I suppose it isn't," I answered. "But I don't have a wife. How would you like to be mine?"

She burst out laughing at the happy thought of the life ahead. How many years went by, one behind the other, pushing their twelve months in front of them?

---

[55] *A highly-prized variety of sugarcane.*

By day I planted the land like my father and grandfather before me, and the land gave me all the treasures from its belly. By night I lay down on the silky pillows of Gracieuse's breasts, drowning myself in the salty water of her thighs, and our children were born, sometimes two at a time, strong and healthy for tomorrow. But happiness is never but a lull in the infinite ocean of unhappiness.

One morning I awoke to the clamor of pigs being slit open. It was Christmas Day and the butchers were wiping their red, murderous hands on bay-rum leaves. The women were washing the pigs' guts in the river. I was sickened by it all, and so I took my hoe and went down to the savanna.

Gracieuse laughed. "You're being silly. Our parents always celebrated Christmas this way. Would you prefer the frozen turkeys in the shops?"

I gave no answer.

At the stroke of three in the afternoon the smell of smoke filled my nostrils. At the same time, I heard a muffled sound like when the gully overflows its banks in the rainy season. I looked up, wiping the sweat from my forehead, and saw the hill in flames. The time it took to realize what was happening, to throw down my tools, and run as fast as I could, my cabin had gone up in smoke, and everything I possessed was reduced to ashes.

The French-French gendarmes did what they'd been told to do. They asked questions. On finding a kerosene drum in the vicinity, they inferred I had enemies. According to them, the entire village hated me for being so fortunate and so happy. Ever since that day, I have dragged my body through the potholes of existence. I have watched this country change.

I watched the whites flee in a great disorder as the plantations went up in smoke. I watched the Negroes jubilantly turn their backs on the stinging cane and crowd into the roads leading to the towns. The women observed them as they went, wiping the tears from their eyes and cradling their bastard children in their arms, knowing full well in the secret of their hearts that this jubilation would not last and that soon poverty would bring them home again. I watched the schools open and, to my disbelief, heard the children chant: "Our ancestors the Gauls . . ."

I watched the coming of electric light. I watched the electric poles go up, the roads tarred, the houses built of concrete and cars running on four wheels. In La Pointe the guppies died of thirst at the bottom of the storm canals, drained of their water, while men's hearts turned hard and wicked, devoured by stereo players and color television sets. When I drew near the villages, the men would pick up rocks to drive me away and the women shouted at me as if I were a dog: "Shoo! Shoo!"

So I ventured out only under the protection of the night when the moon told me the way was clear.

Year after year I watched the banana groves wage war on the mountain immortelles, the tractors replace the machete and the trees of life felled with one blow on a land smitten with alopecia. Where could I hide? Where could I hide? I ran in all directions and the sun hurt my eyes.

One day I emerged from a forest path and some trees called out to offer me their shade. I obeyed and curled up in the familiar sweltering heat of their armpits. I tied myself down with the vines. I suffocated with happiness. As soon as the sun had started its journey to the other side of the world and darkness pressed down on everything, I descended to the bottom of the gully. Hidden under the rocks, I turned into a devil's darning needle to listen to the song of the water.

Rivière au Sel I named this place.

I know its entire history. It was on the buttress roots of its manjack trees that the pool of my blood dried. For a crime was committed here, on this very spot, a long, long time ago. A horrible crime whose pestilential smell stank in the nostrils of the Good Lord. I know where the tortured bodies are buried. I discovered their graves under the moss and lichen. I scratched the earth and whitewashed the conch shells, and every evening at dusk I come here to kneel on my two knees. Nobody has pierced this secret, buried and forgotten. Not even he who runs like a crazed horse, sniffing at the wind and snorting at the air. Every time I meet him my eyes burn into his, and he lowers his head, for this is his crime. His. He can sleep peacefully, though, get his women pregnant, sow his wild oats. I won't touch him. The time for revenge is over.

For Gracieuse, there was no coffin, no wake, no rum, no prayers. No cemetery to lay down her bones in the shade. There were only ashes, black flakes on the charred, black earth. I picked up a handful of cinders. I walked to the beach. Standing under a sea grape tree I opened my hand and the wind blew the ashes over the sea. Ever since that day everything has become muddled in my mind and I've lost track of the days. Do you remember, my love without a grave, when we drifted on the foam of pleasure?

First Light

No sooner had the darkness swallowed up the lanky silhouette of Emile Etienne than the rain stopped. At the same moment the wind got up, not the wind that devastates everything in its despair and disarray, but a soft, caressing wind, smoothing out the rough edges and restoring harmony. It gently pushed the sullen flock of clouds into a corner of the sky and an insidious whiteness began to emerge. It first appeared over in Le Gosier, which is in a straight line across the bay behind a curtain of tall trees. Then gradually it spread and stole across the sky so that in seconds the heavens became a calabash full of milk. The day was going to be dry and clear. Suddenly everyone realized it was five in the morning.

The women, who had left babies with a grandmother or an elder sister, realized the infants would soon be shrieking for their milk, and hurriedly got up. The men, who had drunk for the sake of drinking, looked at the empty rum bottles, realized they were down to the last drop, and got up as well.

So there was a jostle of comings and goings between the veranda and the bedchamber, of genuflections and signs of the cross, of "good-byes" and "What time's the funeral?"

By one of those about-faces that death is capable of, people were having scruples about leaving Francis Sancher lying there in his wooden prison, and they started to pity him.

Léocadie Timothée voiced this reversal of opinion when she murmured:

"Poor devil! Rain like that means he misses being alive, however bitter life was and nothing to sweeten it with."

There was a general sigh of approval, but nobody really knew whether it was for the comment on life or the comment on Francis Sancher. Everyone felt watery-eyed, for what or for whom nobody really knew. People were looking at each other in sadness, suddenly rooted to the spot, incapable of making a move home or starting up the motions of daily life again.

Finally, they reluctantly decided to make a move, wading through the mud while the rain-soaked leaves fell on their necks and stuck there like poultices. Over their heads, the great expanse of sky gradually dried, regaining its usual blue color, and the sun slowly returned to its place in the very middle of the heavens.

Inside the house a devoted group remained behind amid the smell of coffee prepared and served by Marina, Rosa's loving sister. The two families plunged in mourning. The relatives. The friends.

Here especially, the insidious about-face dealt by death and the approaching daylight was working in a wondrous way. Some, like Loulou, or Sylvestre Ramsaran, believing justice had been done, felt purified. Once again they could carry their head high and look people in the eye. Loulou was wondering whether he shouldn't speak to Sylvestre about that piece of land he'd had his eye on bordering the river Moustique, not to set up orchid greenhouses this time, but to plant a variety of grapefruit from Dominica whose flesh was pinker and juicier than those from California. Sylvestre artfully guessed what Loulou would be driving at and was already formulating an offer in his head that would discourage him.

Others like Aristide, Dinah and Dodose Pélagie were close to feeling a kind of grateful affection well up inside them for the man who had given them the courage to discard the old, worn-out clothes they slipped on morning after morning that were too tight around the armpits. Such an emotional upset made them ask themselves questions of a superstitious nature. Who in fact was this man who had chosen to die among them? Could he be an envoy, the messenger of some supernatural force? Hadn't he repeated over and over again: "I shall return each season with a chattering green bird on my fist"? At the time nobody had paid any attention to his words, which had been lost in the ruckus of rum. Perhaps they should watch for him to reappear supreme through the rain-streaked windowpanes of the sky, and finally gather the honey of his wisdom. Just as some of them crossed over to the window to look for the flowering of the dawn, they saw the contours of a rainbow, and it seemed to them a sign that verily the deceased was no ordinary man. Surreptitiously, they crossed themselves.

Shaking off her exhaustion and seeing the wonderfully straight and unobstructed road of her life stretch out in front of her, Dinah opened the book of Psalms and everyone responded.

About the Author

MARYSE CONDÉ is author of *Segu, Children of Segu, Tree of Life*, and *I, Tituba, Black Witch of Salem*, along with several other novels published in French. She is the recipient of the prestigious French award Le Grand Prix Littéraire de la Femme, was a Guggenheim Fellow in 1987–88, and in 1993 was the first woman to be honored as a Puterbaugh Fellow by the University of Oklahoma. She is a professor at the Universities of Virginia and Maryland.

RICHARD PHILCOX is the translator of several of Maryse Condé's novels, including *I, Tituba, Black Witch of Salem*. A

About the Author

recipient of a National Endowment for the Humanities Award, he has taught translation at the Monterey Institute of International Studies, San Francisco State University and the University of Maryland.

Ms. Condé and Mr. Philcox are married and divide their time between the United States and her native Guadeloupe.